MYSTERIOUS WAYS SERIES

BROTHER'S
KEEPER

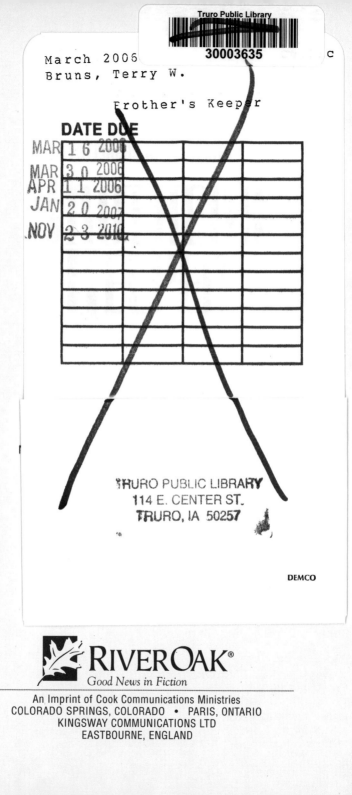

RIVEROAK®

Good News in Fiction

An Imprint of Cook Communications Ministries
COLORADO SPRINGS, COLORADO • PARIS, ONTARIO
KINGSWAY COMMUNICATIONS LTD
EASTBOURNE, ENGLAND

RiverOak® is an imprint of
Cook Communications Ministries, Colorado Springs, CO 80918
Cook Communications, Paris, Ontario
Kingsway Communications, Eastbourne, England

BROTHER'S KEEPER
© 2006 by Terry Burns

This story is a work of fiction. While some characters and events are taken from the pages of history, the main characters and events are the product of the author's imagination. Background events in the story are historically correct. However, license has been taken with the dates of some events to allow them to be used in this story.

First Printing, 2006
Printed in United States of America

1 2 3 4 5 6 7 8 9 10 Printing/Year 11 10 09 08 07 06

Published in association with the literary agency of Hartline Literary Agency, 123 Queenston Dr., Pittsburgh, PA 15235.

Unless otherwise noted, Scripture quotations are taken from the King James Version of the Bible. (Public Domain.)

Library of Congress Cataloging-in-Publication Data

Burns, Terry, 1942-
  Brother's keeper / Terry Burns.
     p. cm.
  ISBN 1-58919-035-1
  1. Twins--Fiction. 2. Farmers--Fiction. 3. Outlaws--Fiction. 4. Brothers--Fiction. I. Title.

PS3602.U7675B76 2006
813'.6--dc22

                                        2005016473

To my brother Trent, who barely made it to forty.
He lived life the way he saw it and,
I suppose, was happy in his way.
I miss him.

I have a friend with agoraphobia, fear of public or wide-open places. The name for the illness did not exist in the time period here, but the affliction surely did. It interested me, and I allowed a character to deal with it in this book.

I also want to recognize long-time critique partner and fellow writer Michelle Buckman, a good friend I intended to recognize in book one of the series but didn't.

One

Cumberland Mountains of Tennessee, late 1860s

*J*ames Campbell ducked to go into the little one-room cabin that had been home his entire life. He caught up a breath at the sight of the stooped, white-headed lady stirring a kettle suspended over the fire in the rock fireplace. *I'd rather take me a beating than to have to tell her,* he thought.

He removed his hat to hold it in both hands in front of his chest, his downcast features saying more than his words. "We're whupped, Ma. That crop is plumb burned up by the sun. It ain't gonna make at all."

She turned an emotionless face toward him. Years of getting by on little or nothing had made hard news nothing new. "This is it then?"

"Yes'm. The bank'll call the note this time for sure. They'll take the place this time." Tears formed in the corners of his eyes.

She wiped her hands on a worn apron and eased herself into the rocker. "I 'spect they will. They've been mighty good to us, particularly since Pa died, but this is the third year of not making money on the crops." She looked around. "They won't be getting much. Not worth what we owe anyways."

He knelt beside her to put his hand on her arm. With a lanky frame that stretched well over six feet, he still looked down on her, even from his knees. "Maybe it's for the best, Ma." His sandy blond hair fell into his eyes, and he pushed it back with one hand.

She nodded. "Probably is. The Lord has always taken care of me. Just hard to leave the only home I've ever known. Can't hardly remember anything before these hills, but we were movers when I was a button. Reckon we're gonna be movers again." The firelight reflected in her blue eyes, a Campbell family trademark, clouded now with a film that often comes with age. She could still see, though not as well as she used to. Still, the eyes were dry; she had long ago used up her tears.

James's head was down. "If only Ross had sent money, the way he said he would." James and Ross were identical twins as far as their physical appearance, but the resemblance between the two young men ended there. Their personalities couldn't be more different. When their father was killed during an argument turned violent, James's immediate reaction was to go console his mother. In stark contrast, Ross grabbed a gun and went to finish the argument.

She now patted James's hand as it rested on her arm. "Don't you go blaming Ross; reckon he's got his hands full just keeping body and soul together. You know when he pulled out of here he was just one step ahead of the sheriff."

James got to his feet, throwing his hat toward the peg on the wall in disgust. He missed. "That's been near two years ago, Ma, and he said he'd help."

"Ross always was a rebellious child, always fighting and scrapping. Always had an eye for what was over the next hill." She knew her boys, their attributes ... their strengths and their weaknesses. They had her unfailing love and support, whether she approved of their activities or not.

The momentary anger gone, James picked up the hat and hung it on the peg properly. "Looks like we're going to find out what's over there for ourselves."

"Looks like."

Mary Jane McMinn worked in the restaurant for her board and keep, if the ramshackle, plank-sided building could actually be called a restaurant, or the little room out back of it could really be considered board. She began to make up the plates for the breakfast orders as she waited for the cook to slap the ham and eggs on them. She wasn't overly fond of the job as it barely provided subsistence, and the restaurant had a reputation as a terribly accident-prone environment. However, an orphan with no family to call on for help couldn't afford to be picky.

Mary Jane paused in front of the mirror to pat her walnut-colored hair into place, then retied her apron strings so it conformed more closely to her shapely figure. Her brown eyes were warm and soft, and she was not displeased with what she saw. She took pride in her appearance and in her work.

She also took pride in keeping the restaurant, and the kitchen, neat and tidy. This compulsion caused her to notice a handle sticking out from a workbench in the middle of the kitchen.

This is the kind of carelessness that causes us to have so many accidents, she thought, as she shoved the protruding handle farther under the bench. On the opposite side of the bench the cook froze in the act of cracking an egg on the hot grill as the other end of the handle suddenly poked between his legs. He emitted a squawk, threw up his hands, and sent the egg flying high into the air.

He bunny-hopped three steps, and in so doing his elbow caught the handle of a pan of fresh gravy, spinning it into the floor. The bunny-hop changed to a frantic flailing of limbs as he fought to keep his balance in the slippery mess. He lost.

Mary Jane heard the cook fall and turned to see him spread-eagled in the floor, squealing in pain as he pawed the air trying to wipe off the remainder of the hot gravy from his face and chest.

"Oh, my goodness," she said as she rushed to his aid and helped him up, tenderly dabbing at the offending mess on his scalded face with a towel.

"Now, now," she said sympathetically in response to his small whimpers. "This is just the sort of thing that happens when people are careless and don't watch what they are doing."

He gave her a dazed look.

"What's going on in here?" the restaurant owner yelled, as he came through the door with a tray of dirty dishes. "Don't tell me there's been another—" his feet slid out from under him as they found the fallen egg. Mary Jane and the cook looked up as time froze, and he seemed to be suspended in the air for a moment. In a strangled voice he cried, "Oh no," and fell like a sack of grain tossed off a tall wagon.

"Umph." They felt the wind, as much as heard the grunt.

They rushed to help him up. He was dazed, unsteady on his feet, but he slowly came around as Mary Jane wiped the egg smear off the back of his pants and dusted him off. "I don't understand," he whined. "It's like living on a battlefield."

"It's her!" The cook pointed a shaking finger at Mary Jane. "It's been this way ever since she came to work here."

"Don't be silly," she said, looking over her shoulder at him. "Just because you two don't pay attention to what you're doing, don't try to blame it on me. I was nowhere near either of you." She didn't understand why people constantly tried to blame someone else for their carelessness.

The owner rubbed his throbbing head. "No, you never seem to be involved in anything that happens, yet there have been an awful lot of coincidences."

The cook was undeterred. "It's her, I tell you. She's a jinx."

"Oh bother," she said. "I'm going to the general store after those things you wanted." She hung her apron on the hook by the door and went out.

"Boss, you gotta do something," the cook pleaded.

"Crop didn't make, Mr. Wilson," James felt like he was on trial as he sat facing the banker across the big desk. The solid brown tones of the office, walnut desk, and paneling were designed to give people a feeling of confidence. But in this instance, it wasn't working. The portly banker had a flushed-red complexion, made more evident by the white pork-chop sideburns that framed his face. The big man was leaning back in his chair, elbows on the chair arms, looking at James over steepled fingers. He liked the boy, had gone further than he should have trying to help him and his mother. Still, there came a time when reality had to be faced.

"I know, James; I've been out that way. I'm sorry, Lord knows you've tried." His sympathy was plain on his face and obviously genuine. "You've been doing a man's work since you were barely tall enough to wrestle the plow. I think maybe God is doing you a favor by relieving you of the burden."

James worried the brim of the battered hat he held in his callused hands. "Yes sir. We've thought on that some." James had dressed up for this meeting, which still meant worn bib overalls, but they were clean and pressed, and Ma kept them mended.

The banker leaned forward in his seat as he

searched for the right words. "If you're here about an extension—"

James cut him off with a palm-out gesture. "No, sir, we can read the handwriting when it's plain on the wall. Ma says to tell you we're mighty beholden to you for all you've done. You've carried us long past where we would have been on our own, and I'm sure the Lord's taken note of it. I reckon the value of our land ain't gonna cover what we owe you."

The banker sat back in his chair. He hadn't wanted to turn James down and was very relieved to have the burden lifted from him. "I'm not worried about that, James, but in fairness to my depositors I can't keep investing their money in business ventures that fail to return a profit." He looked into James's eyes and saw nothing but openness and sincerity. *He might be down, but he isn't beaten by a long shot,* the banker thought. *He'll make it; he just needs a chance, a fresh start. I'll see that he gets that; he deserves it.*

"We know you can't," James replied. "as soon as I can catch on somewhere, I'm gonna send money to make up what our property don't cover."

The banker shook his head as if it pained him, "Please don't even think of it. Your land is just plain worn out, but the bank can afford to let it lay out for a couple of years until it'll produce something. You're going to have enough to do starting over." He stood and offered his hand. "At least you can do it starting clean, not be looking back over your shoulder."

James took the hand firmly and looked directly

into the banker's eyes. "You're a good man, sir. Thank you."

"As are you, James. As are you."

Two

---

*T*he storekeeper nudged his wife. "Martha, it's her."

They looked like shopkeepers. Charles Reynolds had a perpetual pleasant expression that welcomed customers, as did his wife. Martha was short and stocky in counterpoint to his lean, stringy frame. They had lived and worked together for so long that they even finished each other's sentences.

Mary Jane swept into the store with her usual unfailing good humor. Everyone loved her, but things just seemed to happen with her around. Martha whispered, "Oh no," then said out loud, "Good morning, Mary Jane."

"Mornin', Martha. Isn't it a beautiful day?" She handed over the list.

"It certainly is," Martha responded. "Why don't you go on with whatever other errands you have, and we'll get this order filled. I'll send Charles over with it. A pretty girl like you shouldn't be troubled with carrying it." *And it will get you out of the store more quickly,* she thought.

"How nice. Thank you." She turned to leave, then spotted a bolt of material on the counter. "Oh, isn't this beautiful lace?" Mary Jane unwrapped a portion of the delicate material to get a closer look at it. The spool and the remainder of the material dropped over the edge of the counter, falling to the floor with a thud and startling the store cat asleep on the top shelf. Acting as if something were attacking it, the cat exploded down the length of the shelf.

Martha did not see the cat move, and fingering the lace she said proudly, "It's the best we've ever had in here. It sells for twenty cents a yard."

"Mercy, that's out of my price range."

As the cat reached the end of the counter and headed toward the storeroom and the back door, Charles walked past. He was just in time to receive a solid blow in the midsection as he got between the cat and the exit. He emitted a startled grunt but maintained the presence of mind to keep hold of the armload of tomatoes he had been carrying.

It was an act worthy of the circus—the air full of bright-red vegetables, Charles grabbing, catching, missing, tripping, until the result looked for all the world as if he were juggling them.

"I didn't know Charles could juggle," Mary Jane said in wonder.

"Nor did I," said Martha.

"He must really have a lot of confidence to do it with something as fragile as tomatoes. I'd use something that didn't make as much of a mess if I dropped them."

Charles held his own for quite a while but couldn't maintain his success. Even the ones he had captured began to slip. The cat, knocked into the corner by the collision, made another try for the door but failed to negotiate the turn when it hit the mashed tomatoes on the floor. All four feet went out from under it, and screaming a high-pitched howl, the animal slid into Charles' shins, claws first.

Charles recoiled, got caught up in the increasing tomato slime on the floor, and went down hard. The ladies rushed to him. When they looked over the counter, they caught their breath. The mess on the floor resembled nothing so much as a pool of blood, until their senses caught up with the fact that it was tomato juice everywhere, and not blood.

"Are you all right?" Mary Jane asked.

Charles got slowly to his feet, using the counter to keep from falling down again. The cat was long gone, and Charles was unaware of what had provoked the animal.

"Charles, what on earth happened?" Martha asked wide eyed. Such clumsiness was very unlike her husband.

"I have no idea." He had the vacant, uncomprehending look that was often seen on the faces of people around Mary Jane.

"Don't feel bad," Mary Jane consoled. "Things

like this seem to be happening all over town." *People simply do not watch what they are doing*, she thought. "Well, I must get back to work, unless I can do something to help you clean up."

"No!" they cried in unison. Then Martha added, "We'll get it, my dear, I know you have work to do."

"Yes. Very well. I'm sorry for your difficulty."

They watched her exit the store. "She was nowhere near me," Charles said.

Martha nodded dumbly. "No, she didn't do a thing, not a blessed thing. She never does."

From the bank James stepped over to the saloon. He wasn't a drinking man, but if there was a job to be had, the saloon is where he would find out about it. The saloon was more than a place to get a drink; it was communications central, offered the only entertainment in town, and often doubled as a courthouse or even housed the church on Sunday. It was a known thing; when men hit a town, the saloon was the first place they would go to find out what was going on.

As to the church function, James had often wondered whether God was likely to be upset because His people were coming into the Devil's stronghold or pleased because His Word was being carried right into the Devil's backyard. Either way it was too far for him and Ma to come for church, and up in the hills they and their neighbors held services over in Josiah Tomlinson's barn. The Lord didn't seem to mind.

When his eyes had adjusted to the darkened

room, he moved to the bar to order a sarsaparilla. The bartender smiled as he poured it. "Don't see you in here much."

"No, Ma frowns on me coming in here, even if it ain't to drink."

The bartender slid the dark liquid toward him with a smirk. "Ain't you a little old to be letting your mama run over you like that?"

If the comment struck home, James gave no sign of it. "She don't run over me none; I just like to please her. And she's generally right anyway."

"If that's the case, what brings you in here now?" The bartender went back to polishing glasses with the bar towel, glancing up at James as he worked. He didn't tease him further, for in truth, he admired the boy for the strength of his convictions. He knew it would be far easier for him to give in and hang out with the others who frequented his place, but James was too strong for that. Of course, it would be bad for business if everybody were that strong willed.

James wiped the foam from his mouth with the back of his hand. "I gotta find work. We're losing our place."

The bartender nodded knowingly. "I hate to hear that, but there's a half-dozen other boys in here that's looking and ain't finding."

James looked around the room, appraising what he saw. "They're hunting riding jobs—I'd work at near anything."

The bartender tried to appear unconcerned by busying himself wiping down the bar with the towel that had been hanging over his shoulder. "That's admirable, but I don't figure it makes much difference. Ain't no jobs of any kind as far as I know."

James swallowed the remainder of his drink and asked around the room. As the bartender predicted, no one offered him any encouragement. It looked as though a job was not going to be an option.

James put the misshapen old hat on his head to shade his eyes from the baking sun, pushed through the swinging doors, and stepped out onto the boardwalk. He turned, almost running into a shapely young lady. "Pardon me, ma'am. 'Pears I need to get my mind on my business here."

"Hello, James."

He whipped the hat off his head as he recognized her. "I'm sorry, Mary Jane. I don't know where my mind is."

"I know where it is. I've heard." Her chocolate brown eyes telegraphed her concern. They bored into him. It seemed as though everywhere he looked these days, he saw people pitying him. It was becoming rather hard to take.

He gave the usual response. "It's all right; it's been coming for a long time."

Tears formed in her eyes. "You're leaving, aren't you?"

His eyes refused to meet hers. "Farm's gone, and there ain't no work around here. Reckon we got no choice."

Her hand came to her mouth. "But if you go ..."

Ross, James's twin brother, had spoken for Mary Jane before he left town. James knew what was troubling her. "I know. If we ain't here, Ross probably won't ever come back." *Ross ain't ever coming back anyway,* he thought, but couldn't bring himself to say it. If two years of waiting and hoping hadn't dimmed her hopes, it wasn't in him to put it into words.

"What will I do?" She looked stunned, as if his words weren't making sense.

He took a deep breath and grimaced. She left him no choice; he had to say it. "Ross ain't ever coming back, Mary Jane. You're gonna have to let him go."

Her head dropped. Her voice was so low he barely heard: "I can't."

He put his hand on her shoulder, leaned down so he could look her in the eye, and tried to find more words. "Ma's got it in her head to go find him. I reckon there's mighty long odds on that happening, but it's in her to try. She said she can't lie down for her eternal reward without she sees him again."

Her eyes were moist as she looked up. "But you don't think you'll find him?"

"I aim to try. I'll tell him you're waiting for him."

She searched his face, measuring the truth of his words. She saw nothing but genuine concern. "But you don't think he'll come for me?"

James rubbed the back of his neck, finding it suddenly full of tension. "Mary Jane, I just plumb don't know how to say this."

She straightened her backbone. "Just come right out with it."

"I been thinking on it. Ross may have gone and got himself involved in that terrible Civil War we had some time back. He may not be able to write." It was a thought that had been nagging at him, something he had not even shared with Ma, particularly not Ma.

"You mean—" Her hand again went to her mouth, and she said in a low voice, "You think he's dead?"

James felt trapped. This wasn't a conversation he wanted to have. He liked this girl, and the last thing he wanted to do was bring her pain. "Now don't go borrowing trouble; I didn't mean it that way at all. I don't even know that he did go to war, just thought it might be a possibility." He rubbed his chin. "Then again, Ross ain't much for involving himself in other people's troubles." He hadn't had that particular thought before, but now that he did, he knew it was likely true.

She relaxed a little. "No, he isn't." Curiosity registered on her face as if it had never before occurred to her to ask. "Why didn't you go to war?"

He shrugged. "I didn't even know what they were fighting about. Besides, that would have left Ma to run the place alone."

"Yes, I can see that. Oh, I hope he didn't go either. I don't think I could bear it if he was wounded ... or worse."

Three

*I*t was no chore fitting their remaining belongings into the small wagon. James had traded furniture, farm implements, virtually all they had for the wagon and a second mule to help pull it. Though the wagon was old and ugly, it was dependable.

The last things to go on the wagon were the big cooking kettle and Ma's precious rocking chair. James tied up the tailgate, then started filling the big water barrel with the bucket from the well.

Ma tied her bonnet on her head, freezing in the act of tying it under her chin. "Well, I'll be."

"What is it, Ma?"

James turned and looked down the road. Mary Jane was coming over the hill carrying a broomstick on her shoulders like a yoke. Large bundles hung on the ends of the stick, containing clothing and other belongings.

He smiled. "Looks like we gonna have us a passenger."

When Mary Jane approached the pair, Ma put her hands on her hips as she spoke. "Girl, what is it you think you're doing?"

"I'm not sure, Mrs. Campbell. I'm either hitching a ride, or I'm setting up to follow behind the wagon when you leave." She put her bundle down on the porch and sat down heavily beside it, sticking her feet out in front of her and tucking her skirt between her knees. She let out a long sigh of relief to be getting off her feet after the strenuous walk from town.

"And why would you be doin' that?"

She raised her hands in a gesture of resignation, then let them fall back in her lap. "If Ross isn't going to come home on his own, then I suppose it's up to me to go find him. Since you're planning on doing the same thing, I thought we might as well do it together."

Ma frowned. "It ain't seemly, an unattached girl of a marriageable age traipsing along with an unmarried man."

Mary Jane's smile was disarming. "Oh, Mrs. Campbell, I'd be chaperoned, and well you know it. It's not as though anybody is going to miss me. Besides, they're blaming me for all the silly accidents that have been happening at the restaurant. Mr. Tucker let me go."

Ma's features softened. "How terrible. As far as

that goes, neither of us is going to leave as big a hole in this town as a fish leaves in the water when he jumps." She turned her attention to her son. "James, toss her stuff up there, and help her up on that seat."

Mary Jane shook her head as she jumped to her feet. "Oh, I can't sit there; that's your place."

Ma laughed. No sound came out, but her sides heaved as testimony of her amusement. "My place? My place is in my rocking chair in front of that fire in the cabin. Can't take the fireplace, but I intend to ride this rocking chair all the way."

James set the bundles in the wagon as directed, then turned to the two women. "Well, let's us have a little prayer before we head out. I'm thinking we're gonna need a powerful lot of help on this trip."

James and Ma joined hands, then each held out the other hand to Mary Jane. She backed up a step. "Oh ... no ... I don't believe in that stuff."

Ma looked surprised. "Child, are you telling me you don't believe in God?"

Mary Jane held back like a little girl scared of the doctor's office. "I used to, at least I think I did."

"I don't understand," James said as he dropped the hand he had held out to her. His face was full of concern.

Mary Jane shook her head with an exaggerated slowness. "God took my mama and daddy. He even took my baby brother. I don't know that I want to believe in a God that would do that."

"Losing loved ones can test our faith, and that's a fact, but that don't mean God took them from us," Ma nodded knowingly. "We're going to have a lot to talk

about, but *we* believe, James and me, and we're
going to pray for our journey. We'd take it right well
if you'd help us complete the circle, whether you
believe or not." She held out her hand again.

Mary Jane came forward slowly, shyly. She took
their hands and bowed her head as James voiced a
prayer. "Lord, we're thanking You for the many blessings You've given us. Things look a little dark right
now, but we know You're still in charge, and Lord,
we know You have a way of making all things work
together for good. We're just asking You to watch
over us and keep us safe on our journey. I 'spect in
the days to come we're gonna be mighty dependent
on Your love and mercy. Forgive us where we've
failed You, Lord, for we ask it in the name of Jesus.
Amen."

Mary Jane looked at him with puzzlement on her
face. "I don't see how you can thank God for your
blessings after all the troubles you've had."

James helped Ma up into her place. "Oh, God
never promised us that life was going to be a down-
hill pull all the way. We've had good times and bad
times, but the Lord has got us through all of them.
We've got our health, and we've got each other.
Things ain't so bad; we just have to deal with whatever life puts in front of us."

He finished filling the barrel, then hung the
bucket on a peg underneath the wagon.

Looking around, Mary Jane noticed that James's
coon dog, Old Blue, was still tied to the porch. Eager
to help, she undid the long rope and tied it to the end
of the wagon. *Wouldn't do to have him running loose,*

but it wouldn't do to forget him and leave him behind either.

James replaced the top on the barrel, then stopped to take one last look around. He noticed that someone had untied Blue from the post. He saw nothing else left to do.

His eyes scanned the yard, the run-down house, the tiny clearing so tightly ringed with trees. "Never figured I'd miss this piece of dirt, but here I ain't even left the yard, and I'm missing it already." He helped Mary Jane climb up on the wagon seat, then scrambled up beside her. Gathering the reins into both hands, he slapped the mules on the rump, and without looking back again, the small group pulled out.

If a man makes a living with a gun, he gets fast or he gets dead. Ross Campbell was very much alive, and he intended to stay that way. He narrowed his eyes to look at the little man across the poker table from him. The man reminded him of a weasel, with his delicate features and shifty eyes. His hands were white as if they had never seen the sun, with slim, almost feminine fingers.

Ross was fairly sure the man had been dealing seconds, with an occasional card taken off the bottom of the deck. In time, even one of these farmers would spot it, so he figured he would just wait him out. He didn't need the trouble. He didn't plan on the man trying to divert attention away from himself by shifting it to him.

Ross gave a smile with no humor in it as he

spoke, "Friend, you go accusing me of cheating, you'd best be ready to back it up."

There was a scuffling sound as chairs pushed back, and people cleared the line of fire in the dingy little saloon. Everyone knew fighting words when they heard them. The light from a half-dozen kerosene lanterns cast shadows around the room, and the dim glow made each face look hard, serious.

The gambler across the table stood deliberately, resting both hands on the table. "I'm accusing, and I can back my play."

Sleeve gun, Ross thought. From the way the gambler was standing, he would have to turn his wrist and dump the little pistol right into his hand. It was a pretty risky draw with so much at stake. His voice was low and even. "You may be able to back it, but it's a mighty dumb play."

Weasel Man sneered. "And easy to avoid; you just push that pile back out into the middle of the table and walk off."

Ross tried to remember, was the restraining strap off his pistol? Was it free in the holster? He wasn't about to take his eyes off the little man to look, and dropping a hand off the table to check would be interpreted as a draw. He was pretty sure the leather loop was still over the hammer. It always was when he rode; the way his holster rode on his leg, it had to be. "Not going to happen. You ready to die for this pot?"

"I won't be the one to ..."

Ross had known the draw would come in mid-sentence, and as he saw the gambler move his hand, he didn't even bother to rise. He dropped his right hand, thumbed the strap off the hammer of the weapon, and pushed down on the butt of his Colt in one movement, swiveling it upward, holster and all. He fired twice up through the table. He felt the pistol recoil sharply as the flame from the barrel scorched his leg.

The gambler rose up on his toes, a shocked look on his face. He had two bright splotches of red on his chest, framed by wood splinters. He fell forward onto the table, then slid to the floor.

"That was a fool play," Ross muttered as he rose, swept the chips into his hat, and walked over to the bartender to cash them in. He leaned against the bar and half-turned to face the door. *Any time now.*

The sheriff and a deputy clutching a shotgun burst through the swinging doors. "Everybody keep their hands where I can see them." The overweight sheriff was out of breath. The florid red color of his face was probably not all due to exertion. "Who's doing the shooting?"

All eyes went to the stranger at the bar, but nobody answered. The sheriff turned to face him, in a glance taking in his tall and lean frame. His eyes continued down to the set of matched pistols at his side. Ross's eyes were shaded beneath the black flat-crowned hat, but the sheriff could see the menace in them. The sheriff knew this man was trouble with a capital *T.*

"You do this?" the sheriff asked as he walked over to the gambler on the floor. The crowd shifted as he moved, still careful to stay out of the line of fire. The deputy focused the shotgun on Ross and eased the hammers back with a noise like walnuts cracking.

Ross looked relaxed, but his hand hovered near his pistol. He never knew how these things were going to play out. If this one went sour, he would have to take these guys, and the shotgun would have to go first. Even if he got the deputy and the sheriff both, there was no guarantee the good citizens would stay out of it. He was under no illusions about the danger that faced him.

"I did it all right, but I had no choice," Ross said. "Look in his hand; you'll see the toy pistol he tried to use on me. I was still in my chair."

The sheriff knelt and took the derringer from the gambler's hand. He broke it open and saw that it hadn't been fired. "You see it that way?" He posed the question to a couple of nearby men. They were keeping a close eye on the money they had left on the table.

They nodded, and one said, "It happened like he said, Sheriff. The tinhorn tried to use that little sneak gun on this man, but he shot him right up through the table. Durndest thing I ever saw."

The sheriff slipped the little gun into his vest pocket. "All right, stranger, I guess it was a fair fight, but I got to tell you this hombre has relatives out at the Bar Y, and unless I miss my guess, somebody is wearing out a good horse going to tell them right now."

Ross gave a wry smile. "There's always relatives."

The sheriff walked over to confront him. "Always? This happen to you a lot?"

The bartender handed Ross his money. his attention never strayed from the two lawmen. Ross took the money in his left hand, folded it, and tucked it into the inside pocket of his cowhide vest. "It's happened before."

The sheriff narrowed his eyes, measuring Ross, evaluating. He was making up his mind, and Ross knew it. He was poised ... waiting. "If I go back and start going through my circulars, am I going to find your face?"

Ross turned to the bar to empty his drink, making a show of relaxing. He continued to watch the two men in the mirror, still poised to make his play no matter how it looked. He tried to sound casual as he answered. "I'm not wanted in these parts for anything I know of, unless you get circulars from jealous husbands."

The sheriff's grin was barely visible beneath his drooping white mustache. "Husbands aren't that well organized yet, though they probably should be." The deputy let the hammers down on the shotgun, and Ross relaxed.

The sheriff looked over to call out a couple of names. "Sam, Homer, you boys go get that shutter Frankie totes drunks out on and take this jasper down to the undertaker. His brothers will be in to settle up soon enough." His gaze swiveled back to Ross. "Unless they're otherwise occupied."

"Don't rattle your saber at me, Sheriff. I ain't planning on sticking around." Besides that, Ross didn't want to gamble on the sheriff's calling his bluff and going through those circulars.

Four

Y ou know, I don't feel all that bad." James held the reins casually, hands resting on his knees. The mules needed little direction on such an established road. They understood what they were expected to do. They walked, they pulled, and they kept it up until somebody turned or stopped them.

Mary Jane had been passing the time snapping green beans into a bowl held in her lap. "What do you mean?"

"I kinda had a lump in my throat back at the house. I really hated to leave. But I don't know, now, it's more like ... hard to say ... I guess I feel like a load has been lifted off me." It was strange that he hadn't realized he had been under pressure; it was just how things were, but now he felt relaxed, free. It was a good feeling.

"And a big load it was," Ma said from the back. "You never got to be a kid. You've had to be a grown man all your life. I'm sorry about that."

"Don't be, Ma. Didn't mean it to sound that way at all. I've always been content with my lot; only I ain't never done anything different in my whole life. If'n we were still at the farm, I'd keep it up, and do it gladly, but here I am on an adventure, and instead of being scared, it feels good."

"Yes!" Mary Jane said. "I feel the same way. I've never been off the mountain before. This is so exciting!"

"Well," Ma observed, "before you two get too worked up, remember we don't have any idea where we're going, no money, and not a lot of food. This ain't exactly no pleasure trip."

It wasn't that Ma didn't welcome an adventure— she was always up for a new experience, but she had seen a lot of water go down the creek. She took things with a grain of salt.

"Now, Ma, there's no reason to look at it that way." James smiled. "We're going, so we might as well make the best of it."

"The only thing I can't figure," Ma said, "is what made that porch collapse after all these years, just as we pulled out."

"Ain't that a caution?" James said. "I couldn't fig-ure it neither. Old Blue seemed to get tangled up in it somehow. You see anything, Mary Jane?"

"Not a thing, but there's been a lot of that sort of thing going on."

"Well, I got him up here now." He tussled the dog's head and rubbed him behind the ear. "Reckon it's best he ride up here with us 'til we get down the road a piece."

The road led back through town. As they approached it, they saw that a celebration was in progress. They made their way down the street, but people seemed embarrassed to see them, to be caught in the midst of their celebration.

James misinterpreted the looks they received as they drove in. "These folks have been good to us, but I've had about enough of these looks of pity."

"Yes," Ma agreed, "me too. Wonder what they're celebrating?"

James pointed. "I'd say it's a send-off for Mary Jane. Her name is on that banner over the street."

Mary Jane straightened her bonnet. "Well, isn't that sweet?" They stopped, and she got out. She looked at the gathered townsfolk. "I can't believe you all went to all this trouble for me."

The storekeeper flushed red. "Well ... err ... we thought you'd gone." He caught himself. "Isn't it lucky we weren't too late?" He gave a sheepish grin to his wife.

Mary Jane smiled as she touched the store-keeper's arm. "Lucky indeed; we were on our way out of town. We can only stay a minute though."

Charles pulled at his collar. "Good. That is, good that you were able to join us."

James and Ma stepped down from the wagon and were served cake and punch by townspeople genuinely sorry to see them go. Ma looked as if she were about to take flight. She didn't come into town often and seemed to be taken by nervousness and shortness of breath when she did. She thought maybe it had something to do with coming down out of that high mountain air.

The same people expressing reluctance to see Ma and James go watched Mary Jane nervously, as if she might explode any minute.

After a few pleasantries, James said, "Bad as I hate to do it, we've got to get on the road. We're committed now, so we got to get to it."

He walked Ma over to help her up, and Mary Jane walked around to the other side of the wagon. She walked under the banner that said "Good-bye Mary Jane" in large, bold hand-printed letters. It was suspended on a rope across the street, but the bottom ropes hung down loose.

"Oh my, this has come undone." She picked up the trailing rope from the banner and looked around, but the only object she could see that it would reach in order to secure it was an old buckboard. She tied it off, then climbed up on the wagon beside James.

They waved, smiled, and drove out of town to a spirited chorus of farewells.

The cook from the restaurant walked over. He looked incredulous. "Is that it? She's leaving, and nothing happened?"

Charles shook his head. "I don't believe it."

The revelation caused the celebration to erupt in full force: singing, shouting, and patting each other on the back. Shortly a rancher said, "Hate to leave

such a good time, but if the missus finds out I'm having this much fun without her, she'll be fit to be tied."

He stepped up into his buckboard and whipped
up his team. People paid little attention to his departure ... until the rope tied to the buckboard came
taut. It snapped the top rope on the banner and fell
toward a cow pony tied outside the saloon.

Out of the corner of its eye, the horse saw some
giant thing flapping like a deranged bird that
appeared to be coming toward it. Terrified, the horse
began to back up, jerking the top rail completely off
the hitching post. The flopping, flailing post
increased the gross terror of the animal but impeded
it so it could not turn to run.

One wouldn't think a horse could back up at that
speed, particularly dragging a post, but it got it done.
Unfortunately, in that position it couldn't see where
it was backing, or the animal would have surely
avoided the table with the punch bowl and the plates
of cake cut to serve.

Contact with the table brought a squeal of pain,
and the horse lashed out with both powerful hind
legs, overturning the table, sending the pieces of
cake through the air like bats flying out of a cave.
The punch bowl went through the front window of
the bank like a cannonball.

Stunned and smeared with cake, the crowd in the
street turned as one to look after the Campbell
wagon, now far in the distance.

"Wonder how she done that?" the bartender
whined.

Charles grimaced and shrugged. "Our fault. We

shoulda made sure she was really gone before we started celebrating."

The Campbells and Mary Jane weren't the only wayfarers on the trail. Making its way up out of Texas and over into the western part of Indian Territory, another group in two wagons rode patiently along. Amos Taylor, who was wearing the white clerical collar and black tailored suit that marked him as a man of the cloth, drove the lead wagon. He stood six feet two with dark-brown hair that matched the thick fringe under his nose.

Amos hadn't always been a circuit-riding preacher. Not so long ago, he had been a rogue and a scoundrel, preying on the unsuspecting, robbing and tricking people out of their money. But that was before God had taken him in hand.

Amos's wife, Judy, drove the second wagon. She was every inch the lady, with long chestnut hair and soft brown eyes. She had a lot to do with his finding religion, but not nearly as much as had Joseph Washington, the old black man riding beside her. Though blind, he was the preacher's right-hand man, functioning as part-time song leader and full-time conscience. His dark ebony skin made his white hair, beard, and eyebrows stand out as if they were lit up from within.

When Amos had arrived in Texas posing as a preacher to cover his nefarious activities, Joseph had seen right through him and had been struck by a firm conviction that the Lord was using Amos whether he knew it or not. Joseph had not let up on

Amos until he found himself preaching for real.

The trio were now taking a tent revival on the road, and they had started by going back to all the places where Amos had robbed and cheated so he could apologize and try to set things right. Needless to say, this was very dangerous business.

Amos had already been berated, beset, and beaten, but God had preserved him from being killed. Amos had accepted the rough treatment as his due for his former ungodly lifestyle, but more than once he had been narrowly saved from an encounter with a noose.

The three were unaware of it, but they were now making their way toward an ample supply of additional trouble. It would have made no difference if they had known, however, as Amos went where he felt God was leading him to go, and for several days he had felt that the Lord had something for him to do in the direction he was now heading.

Ain't that always the way of it? Ross pushed the little mountain-bred horse out of town heading east. He rode at a brisk pace until he hit Salt Creek, then turned south to ride in the creek, cutting his pace to a comfortable walk. His mind had been set on a good night's sleep in a real bed. *Happens ever' time.*

The horse was fresh from an evening at the livery stable, grain fed, rubbed down, and primed for a long ride. What with misdirecting his presumed pursuers, then riding all night while it was too dark for anybody to track him, Ross calculated that he would be out of their reach by morning. He wondered whether the relatives were partial to that weasel of a gambler or not. If they weren't, they wouldn't be nearly as dedicated about staying on his trail.

Ross had lost track of all the husbands, brothers, and sons who were chasing him for one reason or the other. He didn't worry much about the law. Lawmen generally only gave chase to the end of their jurisdiction, where they stopped, glad to pronounce him someone else's problem.

That wasn't completely true. A Texas Ranger had chased him until they both virtually ran the shoes off their horses. Ross wasn't sure he would ever shake him. One thing he was sure of: If he got away, he didn't figure on going back through Texas any time soon. *Life ain't fair, and that's a fact. How was I supposed to know that old geezer I shot was a state senator? Maybe if I'd killed him he wouldn't been so dead set on sending those badge-toters after me. I bet he put a serious price on my head.*

"I should have stayed back in those Tennessee mountains, horse. Had me a sweet little dumplin' up there that thought the sun rose and set right over my head. What was her name? Don't reckon she was all that special, if I can't even recall her name. I've had better, and I've had worse, but she'd look mighty good to me right now. Don't know how come I never managed to bed her back then; something always seemed to get in the way. Never could figure it."

No such problem with that gal over Abilene way. Now there was a woman. Redheaded, fire-breathing, feisty handful of a woman. She knew how to treat a man.

Getting women had never been a problem for Ross. He and his brother had their mama's clear blue eyes, and his sandy blond hair and boyish good looks brought out the mother in a woman. They all wanted to take him under their wing, and he took full advantage of that maternal instinct.

Ross came up out of the ravine to see two wagons. He rode over to them, and as he got close saw a clerical collar on the driver of the lead wagon. *Bible thumper,* he thought. *Just what I need.*

The last thing he wanted was to have to listen to a bunch of preaching. He had gotten enough of that at home. He resolved to exchange a few pleasantries and move on. Then he saw the woman. She was a real beauty. Maybe he could endure a little preaching after all.

"Howdy," he said when he got close enough.

"Howdy," the preacher answered.

Ross rode over and offered his hand. "Ross Campbell."

The man leaned down to give the hand a firm shake. "I'm Amos Taylor. That's my wife, Judy, driving the second wagon, and my good friend and companion Joseph Washington riding with her."

Ross touched his hand to his hat brim. "Howdy, ma'am, Mr. Washington." He turned his attention back to Amos. "I hate to be nosy, but how come your friend is letting that pretty lady get calluses on her hands when he could be driving?"

"I can see how it might look that way. But Joseph has been blind much of his life. He can do an awful lot, even a little driving when the going isn't too tough, and when Judy's there to serve as his eyes."

"I'm sorry. I didn't know."

"No way you could have. We'd be pleased to have you ride along with us, Mr. Campbell."

Not if that lady is your wife. "I'd enjoy that, Preacher, but I can make a lot better time riding on, and I have some people to meet." He tipped his hat to Judy again. "Nice to meet you folks though."

"God go with you, Mr. Campbell," Amos said.

Yeah, right. Rave on, Preacher.

Five

Staying alive was a full-time job on the trail. James was more than happy that Mary Jane had come with them. She was making things a lot easier on Ma. Traveling with little money and scarce provisions, the trio had two missions: to cover all the miles they could each day before they made night camp, and to be constantly alert for edibles they could use to supplement their dwindling supply of rations. This was poor country, and feed and provisions were hard to come by, although they had seen and gathered a lot of sweet chestnuts during the day. They traveled nineteen miles before they made camp the first night, still in the mountains.

The next day started with breakfast that Ma

cooked on the fire as James tended the mules and hitched up and Mary Jane broke camp. It was fatback and pan bread cooked in a skillet hastily rinsed and stowed at the last minute. James climbed up on the wagon seat, whipped up the mules, and they headed out. They traveled at a comfortable walk, with the women traipsing along on either side of the wagon, scanning the countryside for anything they could add to the cook box.

James drove until they stopped for their noon meal, which was usually little more than hardtack and a pot of coffee, often reheated from breakfast. After noon Mary Jane took over driving the wagon, and James walked out to hunt meat for the pot. He had his daddy's old Hawken long rifle, an outdated flintlock, but unbelievably accurate, and an old double-barrel shotgun. The latter he had bought cheap since it had been rusty with frozen hammers on it. He had spent a lot of hours taking the gun apart, cleaning, oiling, and sanding down the rust. It worked fairly well now, as long as he kept it oiled.

He sorely wished he had a stock horse to ride out on, scout trail, and make hunting easier and more productive. But when a guy was dirt poor, he had to make do with what the Lord provided.

Hunting had been different since they came down out of the high country. Game was more plentiful up in the Cumberlands, and he understood better how to stalk it. As the terrain got lower, the prey was smaller and faster, harder to see in spite of the increased field of vision. But hunting was hunting, and he was a good shot regardless of the circumstances. He wondered what was ahead. More hills? Rivers? *Hear tell there's deserts out here somewhere, and land as flat as the top of a table. Wish I had me a map or at least somebody to ask.*

The Lord soon provided a field full of quail, calling to each other with their distinctive "Bob White, Bob White" call. He quickly bagged several of the fat birds, thinking they would make a nice stew. He saw a small deer, but without his long gun could do nothing about it. He considered that he might have to start carrying both guns in order to be prepared.

He angled back over to the wagon trail, finding that Ma and Mary Jane had already passed by. He followed the wagon tracks to the place where they had already begun to set up camp. They had again made roughly nineteen miles by his calculation.

"Isn't this a nice little pond?" Mary Jane said as he got within range of her voice.

"This looks like somebody's field." He looked around him. It had been mowed and cultivated; it was obvious that somebody had worked it with loving care.

"Yes, it's all right. We met a Mr. Ford, a minister, and he said we could overnight here. It's a little early, but Mrs. Campbell and I thought we'd like to have a little bath before you got back." Her light-brown hair was still wet, making it appear darker than usual. She rubbed it with a towel, giving her a disheveled look. "What nice birds. Give them to me, and I'll pluck them and get them ready to cook while you build a fire."

Ma returned from the pond and got the pot on as

soon as James started the fire. Then he went off to tend to the mules while the women made the stew.

Henry was an old friend of James's. He and the big mule had been tethered to the same plow for nearly half of James's life and most of Henry's days. Solid and dependable, Henry gave a full day's work any time the harness went on. James hung a feed-bag on the animal, then stood talking gently to him, rubbing his neck as he ate. The mules needed feed to supplement their grazing, to give them the nour-ishment to work as hard as would be necessary.

Zachariah was the new mule. He was younger and more spirited than Henry and probably would not have been as steady had he not been hitched in tandem with the more experienced animal.

He pulled against his tether as James approached him, the whites of his eyes showing. Barely broken to harness when James purchased him, he was still suspicious of his surroundings and of James in par-ticular. The jury was still out on Zachariah. He jerked as James hung the nose-bag on him and flinched as James stroked him. He didn't begin to eat until after James had walked away.

James sniffed the air delicately as he finished and walked back toward the fire. "Mmmmmm, that smells mighty good already. I'm hungry as a bear fresh from hibernating."

"We found some wild onions," Ma said. "Nothing smells better cooking than onions do."

He nodded, walked over to the fire for a closer look, and Mary Jane gave him a sip of the stock with a big long-handled spoon. "Coming along good," he pronounced. She smiled and replaced the spoon in the kettle. She stepped away, then thinking better of it, turned and retrieved the spoon. *That gets too hot in there with the kettle on the fire. Mrs. Campbell might burn her hands.*

Not one to waste time, James reached under the wagon seat to retrieve some harness leather he was working on. He pulled out the awl and some strong cotton thread, then walked over to sit on a log by the fire. He punched the awl through the leather and used it to pull the thread back through the hole to make a stitch, then repeated the process again and again.

Mary Jane stepped over to put the spoon in a tin plate on the makeshift table they set up at each stop. She busied herself pouring up the coffee. Ma turned back to see to the stew, wiping her hands on a towel. Finished, she tossed the towel on the table, but it fell short. It caught the spoon handle and flipped it through the air.

The spoon sailed in a high arc as she stood there looking for it in the kettle. It landed on Old Blue's back as he slept under the wagon, causing him to charge out bellowing, right into the faces of Henry and Zachariah tethered to the wagon.

The two animals backpedaled rapidly until they reached the end of their reins, nearly tipping the wagon, jumbling all of the contents of the wagon bed. Henry settled back down immediately, but Zachariah continued to jerk at his restraint, rocking the wagon like a tempest-tossed ship.

"What in the world?" James jumped to his feet

and ran to calm the mules. He walked the reins to Zachariah's head, holding him firmly, talking in a calming voice. The animal was slow to respond.

Behind him, Blue came slinking slowly back, tail between his legs. "Blue! What's gotten into you?"

Ma picked up the offending spoon. "Looks like he carried this off too. Smelled the food on it, I reckon."

James tied the unfortunate hound to the wagon to keep him out of further trouble. He straightened, put his hands on his hips, and tried to stretch the stiffness from the long day's walk out of his lower back.

He looked off at the horizon. "I'd say it's a good thing you stopped early. I don't like the look of those clouds." The entire western horizon was a dark blue, and flashes of lightning lit it up in periodic displays, giant pitchforks spanning the sky, freezing time, then disappearing as quickly as they had come.

"I think you're right," Ma said, looking up. "We'd best batten things down good tonight."

"Yes, it probably has some rain in it." He grabbed a rope and, with the help of Henry, repositioned the wagon so it wasn't broadside to the approaching cloud, but at an angle to it. James reset the stakes on the canvas that served as a rain fly, driving them in firmly.

The wagon was too cramped to provide sleeping quarters for more than the women, so camp life on the trail was mostly conducted under the fly, where they were shaded by the sun or protected from the rain.

By the time they had eaten, the wind had picked

up, so they gathered up the loose items around camp to secure them. The fire burned at a crazy thirty-degree angle. James moved Henry and Zachariah to the lee side of the wagon, where they would be out of the wind, leaving their halters on them and snubbing them tight to the wheel. It was well over an hour to sunset, but it was already getting dark.

The women went to bed in the wagon, securing the flaps at both ends of the cover to close it off. James crawled into his bedding underneath and stretched out.

The wind hit with a sudden savagery. It drove hard, horizontal, pelting rain at them. *This ain't gonna work,* James thought as he crawled out of his bedding. He quickly rolled it and handed it up into the wagon before it got any wetter. "Hand me that coat, please."

He pulled it on and buttoned it to his neck, already sopping wet. He ran to the canvas fly, already loose on one corner and threatening to make a journey into the next county on the wings of the wind. The flailing corner slapped him twice, stinging like blazes before he captured it.

He fought it as if it were a big, furious beast, losing ground, when suddenly Mary Jane was by his side. She grabbed the end with him, and together they took it to the ground. Now the wind helped instead of opposing them, and she used her weight to hold the flailing corner on the ground as he ran to the other corner and released the rope to take it back to the wagon.

Now the wind pinned the tarp to the wagon.

Together they rolled it so it wouldn't catch the wind as much. It was all they could do to keep their feet in the gale. "Get back in the wagon," he shouted into the wind.

"That may not be too safe," she said as she pointed. Gusts of winds raised the wagon up on two wheels, threatening to turn it over with Ma inside.

James reacted instinctively, tying off a rope to a seat support and running it to one of the stakes he had driven to support the tarp. He stretched it out, and close to the stake he tied a loop in the rope. He ran the rope around the stake and back through the loop, then used it to pull the rope against itself, tightening the line. He tied it off, then repeated the process from the back of the wagon to the other stake.

For good measure, James drove two additional stakes and secured the tarp twice more. Mary Jane held the stakes as he drove them. Then he led her to the back of the wagon and hefted her back up inside. He made a quick tour of the camp to secure a few more items. Behind the wagon, Zachariah again danced and kicked. James snubbed both animals tight against the wheel, head-to-head so Henry could help calm the youngster. Then he heard Ma call his name. "James, you get in here."

"'Tain't proper."

"You're drenched; you get in here right now."

He crawled in reluctantly. "Now get out of those wet things," his mother ordered. The women turned their backs, and he stripped down, slipping into dry pants. Ma hung the clothes up at the front of the wagon, and Mary Jane started to towel off his back. It felt so comforting he almost purred. She toweled down his hair as Ma rearranged the bedding. "I'll sleep here in the middle," she announced as she crawled in.

"I'm just gonna sit here a bit and catch my breath," he mumbled as Mary Jane crawled in beside Ma. He nestled into the corner by the tailgate, wedging himself into place and pulling the blanket about him.

Man, I can't believe that little fracas took so much out of me. I'm as tired as if I'd done a full day's plowing.

That was his last conscious thought as his head went back, and he slipped off to sleep. Some time later he felt Mary Jane pull him down flat and cover him up. Her hands were comforting. It had been a long time since anybody had tucked him in.

Six

---

*I*f finding a place to start over was the primary objective for James and his party, just staying alive was a full-time job for his brother, Ross. There was no law in the Indian Territory, at least not out in the part he was entering on his way to what was called No Man's Land.

Back in the eastern part of the Territory were the lands of the Five Civilized Tribes: the Cherokee, Creek, Choctaw, Chickasaw, and Seminole. Their way of life—with villages that rivaled small towns and the use of modern farming methods—was more like that of the whites than the Plains Indians to whose lands they had been forcefully moved from the Southeast by the U.S. government more than thirty years earlier. But on the western end of the Territory, and in the adjacent No Man's Land to which Ross was headed, outlaws and wanted men were rampant. They weren't nearly as afraid of the law as they were of the roaming bands of warlike Comanche and Kiowa warriors.

One thing's for sure, that ranger ain't gonna come over here after me, Ross thought as he forded the muddy water of the Red River. *I'm running shy on cash too. Gonna have to figure out a way to lay hands on some more. The money from that poker game won't last long.*

A nagging thought returned to his mind. *Speaking of money, I promised Ma I'd send some, and I never have.* This wasn't a new idea, but one that passed though his head in a fleeting manner on several occasions. Yet it never found purchase there long enough for him to do anything about it. *Ah, no big thing; she's got that mama's-boy brother of mine there to look after her.*

Ross loved his mother as much as James did, but duty and responsibility had always been a snug fit on him. He threw it off like a tight shirt. He stopped, turned sideways in the saddle, and leaned with his right hand on his horse's rump to get a good view of the river from the ridge.

"Not hard to figure why that's called the Red River," he chuckled. "This whole land's as red as a new pair of long johns." He swiveled back straight in the saddle and tugged his hat back tight on his head. "Horse, you help me watch now. We got to start paying more attention ahead than behind over here. I'm pretty fond of my hair, and the Comanche ride a horse until it's used up, then eat it on the spot. If'n you don't want to end up in an Indian stew pot, you'd better keep a sharp eye out."

Sergeant John David Slocum rode up to a couple of cowhands. He knew he was on the Waggoner Ranch and had been for some time. As he rode up, one of the two men stood and removed a grimy glove. "Ranger, you're a long way from Waco."

"Reckon I am." Slocum was unrelenting on a trail; it wasn't in him to give up. It had earned him the nickname of Bulldog. He reached down to take the proffered hand.

"I'm Mack Steadham," the man said. "I'm the foreman."

"My name is Slocum."

"Bulldog Slocum?"

"Ain't the name my mama gave me, but it seems to have stuck."

"Heard of you." He eyed the wiry little ranger with his full, flowing mustache. The collar-length black hair and mustache on top of skin tanned to leather by the sun gave him a dark, menacing look in spite of the smile he put on. "Thought you'd be bigger."

"Bulldogs ain't all that big neither."

"Now that's a fact. But I gotta say it sure is good to see those badges again. When the rangers broke up and left to become Confederate soldiers, the tribes hereabouts started becoming a problem again. We had our hands full. Wasn't just us, though, I hear tell raiders started giving people fits down on the border too. It hasn't taken long for you guys to start making a difference again. Y'all didn't come back and regroup any too soon."

"Thanks. We like to think we're doing some good."

The foreman pulled off his hat to wipe the sweatband with his bandanna, then his forehead. "Well, that being the case, what'cha doing up this way? You've pert near run outta state when you get here."

"You seen some jasper come through here by the name of Ross Campbell? Tall, lanky fellow, wears two guns?"

Steadham replaced the hat but left it on the back of his head. "Yeah, he come through, all right. Shared a fire and a meal with us at the chuck wagon. Been maybe two days now. I take it you're on his trail?"

"I'd like to talk to the man." Slocum folded his hands on his saddle horn.

"Reckon he's out of your jurisdiction by this time. He asked directions to Doan's Crossing. He'll be well over into the Territory by now."

"The way I see it, that's just another piece of ground on the other side of a river, and I've got time coming to me. A private citizen could drag a man back over here, take his badge out, and arrest him."

"He must have done something mighty bad for you to be dogging him this hard."

"It don't take much. If the boss man says fetch him, I fetch." He gave Steadham another small smile as he added, "He does have a number of things on his circular."

"You don't say?" A puzzled look came over the foreman's face. "Funny, he seemed right nice when he was here. Told some jokes and funny stories and brought us a lot of fresh news." Men who lived a long way from civilization valued fresh news almost as much as fresh food.

"Knew a man once that kept a pet rattlesnake." Slocum smiled. "Said it was good company if'n he didn't make it mad."

Mack threw back his head and laughed, a generous, full-throated sound. "I guess that gets it said." He wiped the corner of his eyes as the laughter subsided. "Step down, Ranger; we've got coffee on the fire."

"Sounds mighty good, but looks like I've got me some time to make up." He reached back in his saddlebag. "But I'd take about a half cup with me and sip on it as I ride, if it ain't too much trouble. Looks to be pretty level around here."

"Sure thing." Mack stepped over to pour some coffee into the tin cup. "If I was you," he said as he handed the cup up to him, "I'd go ahead and take that badge off while you're thinking about it, if you're dead set on doing this."

Slocum accepted the cup and mumbled his thanks. Steadham added, "That's mighty rough country on the other side of the river, and the law ain't exactly welcome over there. If you jump this turkey, you got to figure those folks will side with him, if they figure you to be toting a star. Even if they don't like him."

"Yup, reckon you got the truth of it, all right." He slipped the silver circle with the star in the center into his vest pocket. "Thanks for the coffee and the advice. I'll take it to heart." He reached down to shake Mack's hand one more time.

"I hate to see you go, Ranger. That means I have to get back to work."

"Wondered about that. Don't often see a foreman working like a day hand."

"Men don't expect it, but it ain't in me to just sit a horse and watch others work."

"I 'spect with that attitude you've got a mighty loyal crew. Trust me, you can make book on it. It ain't in cowboys to gush out no emotion. They ride for the brand anyway, like it or not, but they'll do just that much more when they admire the man they ride for as well."

"Thanks, Ranger, that means a lot."

Ross rode up to Doan's Store. It was a small sod building with a hide for a door. Operated by Jonathan Doan and his nephew Corbin Doan, it traded on the fact that it was near the spot where a cattle trail crossed the big river. That made them one of the last supply points before pushing into the Territory. Trail herds, an occasional pilgrim, hands from ranches along the river, and outlaws fleeing into the Territory made up their business.

Jonathan stood behind the makeshift bar and glanced at the lanky man as he ducked under the hide to come in. Doan wondered what category he fell into. "Howdy, stranger, what can I do for you?"

Ross pulled his gloves and pitched them on the bar, raising dust. "Howdy yourself. I could use me a drink of cool water, then maybe a slug of something stronger. That is, if the water ain't out of that river."

Doan laughed. "That'd be like drinking mud. No, we got us a well. Or in a pinch, you can strain that river water through a clean cloth to make it drinkable."

"That's good to know if I get plumb desperate."

"We had to do it ourselves before we got our well dug."

Ross had a drink of the water, then one that was stronger, followed by another glass of water.

Doan smiled. "You were mighty dry."

Ross returned the smile. "I was at that. I was headed up into the Territory for a spell. Anything I ought to know about what's ahead of me?"

The storekeeper thought that pretty well indicated that the man was on the run. "There's a place up north and west of here that's known as No Man's Land. Some Eastern newspaper dude called it that, and it stuck. He said this was 'God's land, but no man's.' It's called that for a reason though. No law up there, so people pretty well take care of things themselves. You on the dodge?"

Ross gave him his sincere, you-can-trust-me smile. "Nothing serious, but I think it'd be a smart idea for me to lay low for a while."

"Good idea to take a little time off now and then no matter what a man's business might be."

"Friend, that's exactly how I look at it. You got anything available to eat?"

"Got a rabbit stew on that's not too bad." Doan went through the hide door behind the bar and returned with a generous-sized bowl of stew and some semifresh corn bread. "Ain't like your mama made, but it'll go down all right."

Ross pulled up to a little rickety table, and Doan joined him as he ate. He pumped the little man for information about the Territory up ahead.

"Ain't nothing but a few scrub cow outfits and a few scarce towns," he said, chuckling. "That is, if you can figure a few sod houses and a catchall store-saloon to be a town. That's pretty much all they are." Doan said it used to be part of Texas.

Ross thought, *If that were the case, ranger would've come boiling after me.*

Seven

The good thing about a nighttime storm is that the countryside generally puts on a fresh face the next morning. The sun broke bright in a blue sky framed by fluffy clouds. The air was fragrant and heady with the smell of all the wet greenery. The light breeze combined with the moisture called for a jacket.

It took a bit of doing to get the wagon trail ready after the big blow. Henry and Zachariah were visibly relieved after the events of the evening, glad to be staked out to graze.

"Mercy sakes but that was a blow," Ma said as she stepped down from the wagon.

"Yes'm, it was for a fact," replied James. He

looked over at the girl arranging firewood for the breakfast fire. "Don't think I could have handled it without Mary Jane. She pitched in at just the right time."

"It was nothing. I could see you needed help." She smiled at the frail little lady. "Mrs. Campbell would have blown away, so I knew that meant it had to be me."

Ma laughed. "How you go on, girl. Isn't it about time you called me Ma? I never had me no girl baby, and I'd kinda like that."

Mary Jane lit up as if she had sunshine on the inside. "Yes'm, I'd be honored, and if we can catch up to Ross, maybe I can make it official."

Ma suddenly felt called upon to busy herself with breakfast preparation. "Well, we'll see what the Lord has in mind on that."

James cleared his throat. He didn't like for Mary Jane to dwell on that subject. "Whether you felt like you were obligated or not, it was a big help, and I'm mighty grateful. In fact, truth be told, you've sure toted your end of the log on this trip. I'm feeling real glad you threw in with us. You've taken a load off Ma—and me as well."

Blushing, Mary Jane waved a hand in a dismissive manner. "Don't go on about it like it was a big thing. I've just been doing what was needed." She busied herself to hide her embarrassment.

James grinned as he saw the red creep into her face. *A woman who can't take a compliment ain't been getting near enough of them.*

Mary Jane changed the subject. "Ma, are you

feeling all right? You seem a little peaked as of late, and the way you've been breathing and sweating makes me wonder if'n you've got a fever."

She went over to place her hand on Ma's forehead. "You don't feel hot."

"I reckon I'm just having trouble getting used to this flatland air. 'Tain't like back where we come from. Seems hard to get a lungful of it."

Slocum rode up to Doan's Store, loosened his cinch, and tied the horse at the rail. He pushed aside the hide door to find a man at the counter. "Howdy, stranger," the man said, pouring a glass of water and pushing it toward Slocum.

"You a mind reader?" Slocum asked.

"Water is always the first thing folks want, then we go from there. I own the place; name's Jonathan Doan."

"I'm Slocum."

"I don't suppose people call you Bulldog, do they?"

"Maybe. You got anything stronger than this?" He held up the water glass.

"Figured you for the law. You know a badge ain't no good on the other side of the river?" He pushed a drink toward Slocum.

"I'm just taking a vacation." He sipped at the water, then braced it with a shot of red-eye. "Whew," he said, "that's not for the young." He wiped his mouth with the back of his hand.

"Make it ourselves. Age it too, unlike a lot of places out here." Doan grinned. "That bottle is pert'near two weeks old."

"Reckon it just disinfected my innards. You seen a character drift through here by the name of Ross Campbell?"

Slocum pushed his glass back toward Doan, who refilled it before he answered. "He came through a couple of days ago. Right nice guy. You a friend of his?"

"Let's just say I'm looking to catch back up to him."

A serious look came over Doan's face. "You right sure you want to go across that river? They ain't friendly to lawmen over there."

Slocum nodded. "Maybe I need me an alias. Reckon if owlhoots can fit a new handle on an old axe, I could do the same."

"You might try Smith. It's real popular this season. You'll find you got lots of kinfolks out this way."

"Smith it is. Could I have a little of that clear water for my canteen too?"

"Glad to be of service, Mr. Smith."

They came down out of the Cumberland Mountains at a place called White Plains, though there didn't appear to be anything white about it. There they found themselves faced with a miserable stretch of road called Bradey's Turnpike. A grizzled old man extracted the outrageous fee of seventy-five cents a wagon to pass.

James and Mary Jane talked as he drove, while Ma dozed in her rocker in the back. The rocker made a comforting squeak, squeak, as it moved with the motion of the wagon. "That old feller back there said we'll be crossing into Arkansas just the other side of Memphis. Have to cross the Mississippi River on some kind of boat or ferry, whatever they have. 'Spect I'll try to catch on to something for a few days to earn us passage and maybe a little money for provisions."

Mary Jane reached into her apron to pull out a small purse. "I've been thinking on that. I've been saving for some time to go after Ross. I was thinking I might have to buy passage on a boat or a stagecoach or a train or something. I've got nearly sixty dollars."

James whistled through his teeth. "Sixty dollars, that's a sight of money, but we can't let you use it on us."

She frowned. "I wouldn't be using it on you. I'd be spending it on my passage, just as I planned. You two have everything you own tied up in this trip, and I need to invest my part."

He looked down at her, studying her face. It was set in resolution. "You sure?"

"Of course I'm sure, silly. That's what I saved it up for."

James turned it over in his mind. It would sure help. But something else occurred to him. "How come you just now bringing it up?"

Her head dropped as if it was something she really didn't want to talk about. "I had to be sure. I had to know you weren't just taking me to some big town to drop me off to fend for myself. I had to have the means of surviving if you abandoned me."

He had a thundercloud look on his face. "You

figure I'm capable of that?" His voice was crisp as he measured his words.

Her eyes were moist as she looked up. "I didn't know. We had barely done more than greet each other in passing. I didn't really know you."

His voice continued to be sharp, "I guess if you're bringing it up now you think you know me better? We ain't cleared that first big town yet. I could still set you and your things by the side of the road."

"I was just being silly, I see that now. You would never leave me stranded; it isn't in you."

I've hurt him. I didn't mean to. "The fault isn't in you; it's in me. An orphan, particularly a girl, has to learn to be very protective of herself. I don't give trust easy, and when I do, I have to be very sure." She put her hand on his arm. "As I am now."

"Well I should hope so."

That didn't fix it. I've got a fence to mend here. He's a good man, and it wasn't right of me to distrust him.

There was empty prairie as far as Ross could see: rolling hills and yellow grass rippling like waves on the ocean. *Except something over there, what is that? A tree? No, too square.* Ross altered his course toward the object. As he got closer, he saw that it was a rough tower. *Must be drilling for water.*

He hailed the house as he got within range. "Hello the house!" A man came out of the door with a rifle in his hands. His painfully thin wife watched from the shadows inside the door, and a towheaded youngster peeked around her legs. Her thin hair was cut short, but she still pushed it back out of her eyes with the back of her hand.

The man was just as skinny, and balding—a family of scarecrows. "Something I can do you for?" There was no welcome in the man's voice.

"I'm peaceable, friend." Ross rested his hands on his saddle horn, purposely far from his guns.

The rifle didn't waver. "Ain't nobody peaceable out here. If it ain't nesters and cowboys shooting at each other over cows, it's outlaws running from the law, taking anything they want. Not that we got anything to take."

"I'm not like that."

The man walked a circle around him, keeping the gun trained. "You wear two guns," he said accusingly. "Working cowboy can't afford that and wouldn't need them."

Ross didn't bother to look as the man passed behind him. "I can use them too, but I never used them on anybody that wasn't a threat to me. You keep pointing that rifle at me, I might start seeing you as a threat though."

The boy ventured out from behind his mother. Ross smiled at the boy. "I think I might have me a piece or two of hard candy in my saddlebag for that button, if you decide not to shoot me. I'm kinda partial to hard candy myself, but I'd share."

The rifle barrel dipped. "I guess you're all right, and the boy ain't had no candy in a long time." The youngster scurried out to take the candy in a grimy hand.

"Step down and water your horse," the man growled.

Ross did as he said, stretching to limber his tight muscles as he set both feet on the ground. He turned to lead the horse toward the wood structure. "Where ya going?"

"Isn't that your well?"

"Ain't got no well. Spring is out back. That's why we built here, good water." He gestured toward the structure. "That's a tower I built. My wife hangs a lantern on it when I'm out so's I can find my way home. I ain't a good judge of time; I tend to let it get dark on me."

"Well, I'll be."

Ross led the animal back to the spring, loosened the girth, and let it drink its fill. He pulled his tin cup from his saddlebags and sampled the spring himself.

"Sweet water," the man said proudly.

"It *is* good."

Ross removed his hat to wipe his forehead, then swabbed the sweatband with his bandanna. He looked at the house; it was made of sod cut into two-foot-thick blocks, with a sod roof resting on a bare framework of spindly timbers.

The man caught him looking. "Ain't much wood around. We make do."

"I can see that. Open windows, I see."

"Can't afford glass, even if I could get it. We close them shutters if it storms. That's mostly in the winter. It can snow sideways here."

"Hard life."

That drew a frown. "It's all ours."

Ross quickly changed the subject. "I hear there's some places that pass for towns out here."

The man cradled his rifle in the crook of his arm. The youngster now looked around his legs, sucking loudly on the candy stick. "'Pass for' would be saying it right; biggest I guess is Beaver City over on the Beaver River. I 'spect there are several hundred people there now. Carrizo is that way."

He made a desultory point. "It's got three saloons and what they call a restaurant. Just a lunch counter actually. Was where the Cole gang hung out."

Ross caught the inflection on the word. "Was?"

"They took 'em out to the cottonwoods down on the river and hung 'em, 'leven of 'em. Well, not Bud Cole—he got away."

Ross put an involuntary hand to his neck, his bandanna suddenly feeling uncomfortably tight. "What'd they do?"

"Anything they thought they could make a dollar at or get away with."

"I thought men on the run hid out up here?"

"Lot of them do."

"But the law came up here and got these guys? I wasn't expecting to hear that."

"Nah, not the law, the people that live there. People pretty much leave folks alone if'n they don't go to killing and thieving up here. Animals don't soil their own den, you know? People oughta do the same. Back that way fer example is a place called Sod Town. The Chitwood gang hangs out there, steals anything with four legs, but they don't bother their neighbors, so they're left alone. They make lots of 'shine too. Sell as much to the Indians as they drink."

"Thought selling whiskey to Indians was illegal."
"You ain't been listening very close."

Eight

Slocum had been seeing the light for some time, as he rode toward it. In a place where there was no light at all, even a small one could be seen from a long way off. As he got close, he was surprised to see it was a lantern hanging on some kind of tower. Over to the left of it stood a house. He hailed it. "Hello the house!"

A rifle barrel poked out of a firing hole. "Who is that?" a female voice asked.

Slocum rode into the light, removed his hat so it wouldn't shade his face, and put his least menacing smile on his face. "Nobody to fear, ma'am. I'm a Texas Ranger, just passing through."

"Anybody could say that."

He pulled the badge out of his pocket and held it up for her to see. "Yes'm, I reckon they could."

"That badge isn't any good over here."

Slocum still talked to a closed door. "No, ma'am, I get told that a lot, but I'm still looking for a man. He's lanky, good natured, and I have reason to think he came this way. I'm looking to catch up to him."

"You a friend of his?"

He slipped the badge back into his pocket. "I've got a message for him."

"Well, he come through, better'n a day ago."

"I'm obliged, ma'am."

"I have that light up to guide my husband in. I can't open up until he comes."

"I understand, ma'am."

"Reckon you could bunk in the barn 'til he does; there's feed and water for your horse."

"I appreciate it, ma'am." He turned his horse toward the small lean-to she was generously calling the barn. There seemed to be fresh hay in it. That would sure beat camping out on the open range.

They had been making eighteen to twenty miles a day since they got down on the plains. It had been cloudy, which afforded them very comfortable conditions in which to travel. They passed through a little town called Dickinson's Springs, but there wasn't much there. They camped outside of town. The next day was the Sabbath, so they wouldn't be traveling.

Mary Jane looked puzzled when they got up and didn't seem to be preparing to move on. "We don't travel on Sunday?"

Ma smiled. "Lands, no, girl. The Good Book says the Sabbath is a day of rest, for us and for these mules. We'll get to go hear a little preaching, so let's get gussied up."

It was a small church, but it had a real organ, powered by two towheaded youngsters pumping it in back. The Campbell party enjoyed the singing, but when the minister went to work, Mary Jane squirmed as if she were wearing a hair shirt.

As they came out later, Ma said, "I swear, Mary Jane, I thought you had ants moving around in your undergarments."

She laughed. "No, it's just a bit uncomfortable being back in church again. It's been a long time."

They walked at a casual pace back toward camp. James lagged behind, probably milking some local for directions and information on what lay ahead.

"And you don't know why it feels like that?" Ma asked Mary Jane about her discomfort in church.

"No ma'am, I don't."

"That's how the Lord works on your heart, girl. He's a-dealing with you. You need to start figuring out what He wants."

Mary Jane stole a glance at her. "How am I supposed to know that?"

"Keep your mind open. Spend some time reading the Bible. He'll tell you."

Mary Jane didn't look convinced. "I'll try. I'm glad we'll be moving on though. I'd rather not have to go back to that church again."

Ma laughed. "Don't be silly. It wasn't your fault

that man got tangled up in your umbrella and tossed the collection plate all over the crowd."

Mary Jane laughed with her. "I didn't even know it was sticking out. It was rather funny when the change hit the man that was sleeping though, wasn't it?"

"I think he thought the Spirit had moved him, the way he leaped to his feet, yelling 'Yes, Lord! You preach it, Parson!'"

Mary Jane nodded. "It would have made more sense if the parson had actually started preaching."

Slocum used his hat to knock the dust off as he entered the rough-plank building that purported to be the saloon, general store, and probably the court-house. The bar was no more than rough planks laid across two beer barrels. He turned the corners of his mouth up in a slight smile as he looked up at the greasy, snaggletoothed bartender and said, "I'm getting this dust off my clothes, can you do anything about the dust in my throat?"

A wide grin with few teeth in it came off as somewhat less than welcoming as the barkeep answered. "I could ram my fist down there with this bar towel and swab it out if you want."

"Very funny," Slocum said. "I think I'll just wash it out the conventional way. I don't reckon you have any cold beer?"

The bartender laughed and drew him a glass of the tepid brew.

"I thought not. Well, here's to looking at you, or maybe it'd be better to drink to not looking at you." He took a long pull and made a face. "It's wet anyway."

"Nine times out of ten."

"I don't wanna know about that tenth time." Slocum made a production out of wiping his face and neck, then his sweatband, with his bandanna. He replaced it and looked up. "You in here all the time?"

"If it's open, I am. I'm the bartender and the swamper, and I also own the place."

"Guess you'd know if a guy by the name of Campbell was around, or had been. Lanky fellow, blondish, wearing two guns?"

"I'd know, and he ain't been."

"I'm gonna cut a circle over this way. If he shows up, I'd give a bright new twenty-dollar gold piece if you'd lock him up in your storeroom for me."

The bartender looked suspicious. "You the law?"

"My boss is mad at him. I was sent to fetch him back." Slocum didn't feel obliged to admit that his boss was the state of Texas.

"I ain't keen on the idea of going up against some hombre that wears two guns, most people that do that know to use them."

"Why would you want to do that? Never saw a barkeep that didn't have some knockout drops behind the bar that'd put a feller out for a few hours. That'd be plenty of time to get him trussed up like a calf for branding."

"I'll think on it."

Ross pushed through the swinging doors. He stopped, holding the doors at arm's length, letting his eyes get accustomed to the dimness. He walked over

to the bar, put a boot on the board that served as a
foot rail, and said, "I'm might' near dry as that dust
out in the street." He tossed a coin on the bar.

"This swill will cut that dust, but I ain't bragging
about what it'll do to your innards."

Ross tossed down the drink in one gulp. The bartender set a mug of beer on the bar without being
asked. When Ross spoke, the first couple of words
came out hoarsely, "Whew, don't spill any of that on
the bar; it'll eat right through it."

"You think you're kidding." The bartender
rubbed his chin. "Your name wouldn't be Campbell,
would it?"

Ross froze with the mug halfway to his mouth.
His free hand went to his left gun. "Why do you want
to know?"

The big man leaned forward on meaty forearms.
"Friend of yours was in here asking about you. Said
he has a message for you from home."

Ross sat the mug down to pour a little water from
a pitcher on the bar on his bandanna. He bathed his
face and neck with it. "He give his name?"

"Smith."

"What'd he look like?" He didn't want to put the
wet bandanna back in his pocket, so he tucked it into
the back of his gun belt to dry.

"Not a big man, black hair and mustache; looked
like he was made out of leather."

"Slocum."

The name surprised the bartender. "The ranger?
He weren't wearing no badge."

Ross let ought a big sigh. "I can't believe he came

all the way over here after me." He ran his hand through his hair. This was going to change things for sure.

The bartender was thinking the same way. "Mister, you got Bulldog Slocum on your trail, you got a peck of trouble. He offered me twenty bucks to lock you up in my storeroom 'til he come back, were you to show."

He looked steadily at Ross. He measured him down to the shiny brace of pistols on his hips. He smiled his ugly smile. "There be easier ways to make twenty dollars."

Ross tossed a gold piece on the counter. "Here's ten for nothing—nothing but telling me which way he rode out."

"He drifted west."

Ross tugged his hat back into place. "That makes east look pretty good to me."

"That's how I'd figure it were I you, which I'm glad I ain't."

Nine

Ross had no idea how long it would take for Slocum to ride the circle he was talking about, or if the shifty bartender was serious about not wanting twenty bucks. He thought it best not to tempt fate, so he rode on.

The day was starting to fade before he saw the campfire and altered his course to ride toward it. "Hello the campfire!" he called out as he approached.

"Hello yourself!" a man called back. "Come on in if you're a mind to and if you're peaceable."

"Friend, you never met anybody so peaceable."

"That why you wear them two shiny pistols?"

"I find it helps keep things peaceful."

"You got a point there. Help yourself to some

coffee, and there's some stew in that pot."

Ross rode to the picket string and tied up his horse. Even before he stepped away from his horse, the odor hit him like a sledgehammer. Hide hunters. The smell of decaying flesh and drying blood turned his stomach. He pulled his coffee cup out of his saddlebags, but even before he approached the fire, he knew eating was out of the question.

Ross knelt by the fire and poured some coffee, mumbling his thanks. He began to blow on the strong brew, grateful that it smelled so strong that it helped cut the smell if he held it right under his nose, which he fully intended to keep doing.

"There's a bowl there for the stew," the big man said. "My name's Haggerty. That there's Gustafson sleeping under that wagon. Don't worry about waking him up, he can't hear it thunder when he's asleep." He didn't offer his hand but remained seated where he was, for which Ross was deeply grateful.

"My name is Campbell, and I thank you for your hospitality, but I ate in the saddle. Didn't expect to meet up with anybody."

"That so? Well, you're welcome to drag your blanket up to the fire for the night."

"That's right neighborly of you, but I'm in something of a rush right now. I'd best have my coffee, then get back on the trail."

"Dangerous trying to ride at night. Good way to cripple a horse."

"Got a bright moon tonight. I figure I'll be all right if I take my time."

"You on the run?"

"Just in a hurry to get somewhere."

Slocum could smell the occupants of the wagon long before he got to them. *Hide hunters*. The smell of blood and buffalo guts had seeped into their pores. No matter how they scrubbed, it took months for it to wear off.

"Howdy, boys, you headed back?" Slocum asked casually.

"You taking a census?" The driver of the wagon had a flowing gray beard that reached down to the middle of his chest with hair the same length trailing down his back. The other man was fat, with a two-day growth of his own. Slocum rode around to the upwind side of the wagon. They noticed the move and laughed.

"I say something funny?"

"Nah," he extended a hand. "My name's Haggerty. This old fool's Gustafson. Don't bother to talk to him; he's deaf as a post."

Slocum shook the hand, resisting the impulse to wipe it off. Haggerty said, "You didn't answer me about taking that census."

"Just lookin' for somebody," Slocum answered. "Wondered how long you'd been out."

"Feels like half my life. Who you huntin'?"

Slocum gave a description of Ross Campbell.

Haggerty spat. "Seen him. He didn't hang around long. Delicate sensibilities I reckon. We know this rig can be a mite fragrant."

"Not to mention us," the little bearded man contributed.

"I thought he couldn't hear."

"Can't hear worth a hoot, but he reads lips pretty good." He hit the old man with his hat. "Anyway, that feller drunk a cup of coffee, filled his canteen from the water barrel, then thanked us, and rode on. Seemed like a real pleasant sort. Didn't understand him being so dead set about riding at night less'n somebody was hot on his trail. He wanted for something?"

"Just need to talk to him. You recollect which way he went?"

"Headed out of here going west," he grinned and pointed, "but that ravine over there ain't as deep as he thought it was. I seen his hat go back east after he dropped out of sight. I figure he was in it."

"You could be right. I ain't seen many hats ride off by themselves in my day." Slocum rode off himself, leaving the two of them laughing. It didn't seem to take much to entertain them.

The closer James and the ladies got to the Mississippi River, the more beautiful and fertile the land got. It was sparsely timbered, almost prairie. The country was now full of livestock feed and provisions, so the market was glutted. Those who lived near the roads made their money off the travelers. If the travelers bought a bushel of corn for the mules early in the morning, they could get it for fifty cents a bushel. Late in the evening it would cost a dollar since the sellers knew they had to have it if they wanted to feed the animals that day.

They soon learned that a little detour of only a

mile or two off the road would mean they could buy corn for twenty to thirty cents a bushel. They found a place to camp well off the road as well.

Ma began to prepare a meal, and Mary Jane filled the lantern with kerosene. As it was nearly full, she sneezed, spilling a substantial amount. She put the cap back on, contemplated wiping it up with a dishcloth, but was afraid they would taste it in their food.

Hands on hips, she looked around. *The old catalog we use when we walk out to relieve ourselves. Of course, perfect.* She tore out several pages to use to sop up the fluid and wipe down the lantern. She scrubbed her hands until they were raw to get the odor off before she started peeling potatoes for supper.

After supper, James picked up the lantern and went over for the catalog, as he prepared for his evening constitutional. He picked it up, noticed some loose pages lying beside it, and took them instead. "Come on, Blue, you wanna stretch your legs?"

They walked out of sight of the wagon, and James squatted down to take care of business. Blue lay close by, waiting. It wasn't very comfortable, certainly not something James desired to linger over. He was soon ready for the papers, but he couldn't find them. He reached over for the lantern, looking around him. As the lantern passed over the kerosene-soaked paper, a spark ignited the fumes, and the papers went up like a photographer's flash pan. The flames singed James's eyebrows, and his recoil caused him to sit back.

"Aw, man, I don't believe this." But his disgust was short lived as it dawned on him that the papers had caught the grass on fire. It was spreading, and spreading fast. He hiked up his pants, pulled his suspenders over his shoulders, and ran for a shovel.

"Fire!" he yelled, grabbing the shovel. The ladies ran with him, and they had their hands full, beating the fire with horse blankets and throwing dirt on it with the shovel. Still it licked at new grass, greedy, spreading.

Ma's skirt caught fire, and James and Mary Jane ran to her to smother it with the blankets. They turned back to the task as soon as they were sure she wasn't hurt.

The cloud of dirt they raised combined with the thick smoke was enough to choke them. They wet down their bandannas and tied them over their noses.

It was two hours before they stumbled back to camp to collapse exhausted, all but James.

"What happened?" Ma asked him.

"I have no earthly idea, Ma. I just know it happened before I got my cleanup work done, if you'll pardon me being crude about it. I got to go get it done now." He turned up his nose. "Whew, these pants are gonna have to be washed."

He disappeared into the darkness. "That boy is getting accident prone," Ma observed.

The trio met a man on the road driving a spring wagon with some groceries in the back. James pulled up and leaned over the side to wave him down. "Good day," the man said. "Can I do something for you?"

"Yessir, we ain't never been in these parts before. Can you tell us where we'd find the nearest wagon yard?"

The man swiveled sideways in the seat and put a foot up on the footboard. "Sure can, you just bear right when you hit the edge of the next town, and you'll find it laid out next to the depot."

That word didn't register, and James had a puzzled look as he asked, "What's a depot?"

The man laughed. "That's a place where the train stops to let off passengers and freight?"

"What's a train?"

"Is this some kind of joke?" One look at the trio on the wagon told him it wasn't. He sighed. "A locomotive is a big engine powered by steam, and it's so strong that it can pull a bunch of what they call railroad cars. When it pulls them, it's called a train. You people don't get around much, do you?"

"We're from up in the Cumberland Mountains. We ain't had no dealings with any trains. They had a steam engine at the sawmill, but it didn't pull nothing, jus' sat there and powered blades and such."

"Same principle."

"Where do we find this depot?"

"You just follow that railroad track over there. Like I say, it'll bear off to the right on the outskirts of Memphis." Anticipating James's next question, he said, "Tracks are what the train runs on."

"So that's what that is." James looked over at Mary Jane, wonder on his face. "We've been talking about that thing for a spell. We couldn't figure out anything that could be that long except a fence, and it's powerful low down for a fence."

They drove off, leaving the man nearly paralyzed with laughter. James said, "That feller sure has got a good sense of humor."

"Reckon he does," Ma said, "though I admit I didn't get the joke."

"Must be a city feller joke."

They followed the tracks until they came to a yard with a number of wagons arrayed around it. Across the yard from the wagons was a red building. It had a porch running completely around it, with benches, boxes, and barrels on it. But they scarcely saw the building, for sitting next to it was a shiny black locomotive with bright-red trim. The large smokestack had a cone on top of it, and steam occasionally spewed out near the bright-red wheels. It was magnificent. James couldn't take his eyes off it.

"Ain't that a caution? Reckon that's the train that feller told us about."

"Wish we could see it move." Mary Jane shared his amazement.

As if on cue the smokestack began to spew smoke, and the giant beast started to back up to couple some cars. "Would you look at that," James pointed, unable to contain his excitement. "Like the man said, it's pushing them cars like they were nothing."

They sat and watched the engine going to and fro, doing its work, before they could tear themselves away and claim a place in the wagon yard. They set up camp, met a few neighbors, then James ventured forth to find out about Memphis.

"While you two get settled in, I reckon it'd be a good idea if I kinda strolled down into town so I can find my way around. And I'd like to make sure it's safe for womenfolk before you and Mary Jane go in to shop." *Who knows what life might be like in such a big place?*

James walked into the business district slowly, finding things of interest everywhere he looked. He turned a corner to see a white man beating a black man who was bent down, trying to shield himself with an upraised arm.

James took several quick steps to grab the man's arm. "Hey, mister, I think he's had enough. He ain't fighting back or nothing."

The man looked back at James over his shoulder, still holding his victim by the shirtfront. He jerked his arm out of James's grasp. "Stranger, are you some kind of darkie-lover or something?"

"I don't know what that is."

The man turned to face James, his face dark with anger. "You'd better find out what it is, and you'd better get to figuring out which side you're on."

"Side? I didn't know we was choosing up sides."

"If you're taking a colored man's side, you're choosing for sure."

James scratched his neck. "You mean having a black skin puts him on one side and white folks on the other side?" James considered himself a reasonable man, and this wasn't adding up for him.

The man turned to face James, letting the frightened Negro scramble away. He took a wide stance, telegraphing trouble. "It certainly does."

"Why would having a colored skin make him different from us?"

The man thought James was having fun at his expense, but if that was the case, he looked mighty serious about it. "Are you telling me that's the first darkie you ever saw?"

James lifted both hands in resignation, letting them fall again. "I don't know what that word means either. It's like you people speak a whole new language here. Still, if that word means a man with a black skin, weren't none of them lived up in the hills where I come from."

The man jabbed a finger in the air toward James. "You'd better get your feelings about them straight. Somebody else might not be as patient with you as I've been."

"Mister, you poke at me with that finger again, and you're gonna lose it. Reckon you might be looking for a fight, and if that's the case, you just jump any time you feel froggy. You'll find I ain't as easy to beat on as some little man laying down not protecting himself."

"Don't you think I won't do it."

James balled his fist and took a step forward. "I do think you won't do it. I think you ain't got the stomach to face a man your own size."

The man backed away quickly, pointing his finger again. "You haven't heard the last of this."

"You come on back if you can work up the nerve."

"I think you made an enemy," a woman's voice said.

James turned to see a lady standing off to the side. "It's not my first. You know what that was all about?"

She began to twist her apron nervously in her hands. "I'm not sure. Several policemen came by while ago, and some Negroes stepped off the sidewalk to let them by. The policemen followed them, you know, like they were herding them. One of the Negroes fell, and a policeman tripped over him. The rest of them drew their guns, and one of them hit the man that was down so hard that he broke his gun."

"Broke his gun, are you sure?"

"I'm very sure. The man you tangled with saw this one and ran half a block to knock him down and beat on him. I don't know what's going on."

"Don't make no sense to me."

"Me either, but I'm going inside where it's safe."

"Good idea. With all this craziness I'd best get back and keep an eye on Ma and Mary Jane."

Ten

Ross rode into what passed for a town, though no sign proclaimed it. There were a couple of dugouts and a building that was mostly tent, with a plank front that had a faded sign that said "Saloon" on it.

He dismounted and went in. A sign indicated there were sleeping cots in the back, and a sampling of dry goods stood on makeshift shelves beside noxious-looking local alcohol behind the bar.

Ross looked around. "Where am I?"

The proprietor looked up with humor in his eyes. He had teeth missing in front, which seemed to make him incapable of using the letter S. "You th-uffering some kind of memory lo-th?" He wore a dusty black derby and a faded shirt and had a towel on as an apron.

"No, just wanted to know the name of the town."

The man tossed the question over to three cowboys who were playing cards at a beat-up table. "We ever get around to calling thi-th town anything?"

They scratched their heads in unison, pondering the question. "Not as I recall," one said. "It's your place, maybe it should be called Osborne."

"That-th good a-th any."

"Your name Osborne?" Ross asked. "I'm Ross Campbell."

They shook hands perfunctorily. "Howdy, Ro-th. Th-umpthing I can do you for?"

"A drink. And some work, preferably something easy but profitable."

He poured the drink. "That'll be a dime. Boy-th over there are in the e-thy but profitable b-uthineth." He spit each "th" until Ross had to fight the urge to pull out his bandanna and swab his face.

Ross tossed down the drink and made his way over to the table. The bandanna came out. "Man can get a bath talking to Osborne very long," one of the men observed.

"I'd say that's a fair statement. He says you boys are in the 'easy work, but good money' business."

The cowboy swore and tossed in his cards. The others seemed to be content with him as the spokesman. "If you consider herding a few cows whose ownership is a little questionable in that category, we might be." He nodded over to the empty chair.

Ross took the chair, dipping from his dwindling resources to buy into the game. "Don't sound too hard to me."

"No, it ain't hard. There's safer work though."

The hand ended. Ross joined in as they threw their ante out into the middle of the table, then watched as the greasy cards were distributed. He fingered the cards gently, noting that there was grease in different places on various cards. He was probably the only man in the game who didn't know what all the cards were clear across the table. He thought it would be advisable for him to bet conservatively and try to keep his losses to a minimum while he fished for information. "I could use the money."

"Couldn't we all? I'm Scott, this is Jack, and that's Wilbur. Last names don't mean much out here, so if you need us to have one, you pick it out for yourself."

"What's the game, Scott?"

"Five-card draw."

"No, I mean how we gonna make this money? What's the deal on the cows?"

"We're gonna ease back over into Texas and help ourselves to a few XIT cattle. Folks ain't particular what brand is on beef over this way."

"I thought he had a lot of hands that watched them pretty close."

"He does, but they just had a fire that got dangerously close to the main house, and all hands had to go fight the fire."

"When did that happen?"

"As soon as Slim gets back here to tell us it's

burning good." He swore again and tossed in another hand. *Apparently some of these guys cheat better than others,* Ross observed.

The following morning, James sat chuckling, reading the newspaper he had picked up in town. The masthead was emblazoned with the title: *The Memphis Daily Appeal.*

"You might let us in on it," Ma said.

"Mary Jane, if you're ready to give up on chasing Ross, there might be other opportunities here."

"I don't understand."

"Listen to this: 'A gentleman, twenty-five years of age, fair personal attractions and moderate income, wishes to make the acquaintance of a young lady with a view to matrimony. The young lady must be of medium height, handsome, intelligent, and educated. Wealth, although not objectionable, will not be considered essential.'" He looked over the page to find her giggling. "You want the address?"

She made a face at him. "No, the intelligent and educated phrase rules me out."

"You certainly fit the medium height and handsome part though. All right, if that doesn't work, how about this one? He's an officer, a major. It says, 'A young gentleman of amiable disposition, wealthy and accomplished, desires to make the acquaintance of a beautiful and interesting young lady, with an ultimate view to matrimony. Appoint an interview.'"

"'Beautiful and interesting' rules me out on that one."

"I disagree. One more then: 'A young man, native of South Carolina, twenty-five years of age, dark hair and blue eyes, who had been in the service in Virginia for two years, but is now exempt from further military duties, wishes to procure a partner for life. All communications strictly confidential. This is a bona fide offer.'" He looked up from the page. "Education is not a problem for this fellow."

"That one is certainly less picky, but I think I'll just stick with Ross."

"Land o' Goshen!" Ma said. "Advertising for women in the newspaper as if they were livestock. What's the world coming to?"

"It's a new world, Ma. Have to go with the times. Well, look at this." He began to tear out an article from the paper.

"What is it?" Mary Jane asked, smiling. "I'll bet it's an advertisement from a young lady looking for a marriageable man."

"Don't seem to be any of those. Might have a use for this though; it tells how to make harness blacking. Says to take common yellow beeswax, about an ounce and a half, four and a half ounces of mutton suet, half an ounce of turpentine, and three ounces of ivory black. Supposed to melt the wax in a vessel over the fire, then add the suet, pouring in the turpentine when both are melted. Then take it off the fire and stir in the black, keeping it stirred until it cools. Says it's to be used with a brush and is not only suitable for harness, but is excellent boot blacking for boots and shoes."

"What do you need that for? You don't shine your boots."

"I might decide to go courting. I'd need to shine them then." He threw back his head and laughed. "Never mind, I've found some much more useful information. Listen to this: 'Sut Lovengood, with whose quaint sayings many of our Tennessee readers are familiar, explains the effect of a first kiss.'"

"A first kiss?"

"The very same. Let me read you what he says about it: 'I happened to pass next day; of course I stopped to enjoy a look at the tempter, as she was mighty lovin' to me. She put wun arm 'round my neck and tuther wun whar the curcingle goes 'round a hoss, tuck the inturn on me with her left foot, and giv' me a kiss! Says she, "Sutty, my love, I've got somthin' for you—a new sensation!"—and I believed it, for I began to feel it already. My toes felt like as ef minners war nibblin' at 'em—a cold streak run up and down my back, like a lizard with a turkey hen after him in sittin' time, and my stummick was hot and onsatisfied like!'"

Both women flushed with color. Ma snorted, "Why would they write a thing like that in the newspaper? Disgraceful."

"It's a joke, Ma."

Mary Jane agreed, "It's terrible, and the grammar is atrocious."

"He's just trying to write it the way some bumpkin might talk. Don't take it so serious."

"Is there anything in that newspaper about that affair in town?" James looked up to see that the question had come from an older man in his shirt-sleeves, a suit coat thrown over his arm. The other hand carried a black bag. James got to his feet. A doctor commanded respect.

"No sir, that's why I got it, but there's nothing in here about it."

"Sit, man, don't get up on my account." He stepped over to a crate. "In fact, I'll join you for a minute if you don't mind."

"No," James said. The doctor looked startled. "What I mean is, that crate is dirty," James continued. "Sit here, sir."

He complied, extending his hand before taking a seat. "I'm Dr. McGowan."

James took the hand. "Honored, sir. I'm James Campbell, and this is my mother, Emma, and our friend Mary Jane McMinn."

The doctor removed his hat, revealing beautiful silver hair. "Charmed, ladies. I'm not taking your seat, am I?"

Ma wiped her hands on her apron and shook his hand as if she were pumping water. "Howdy, Doctor, we're busy boiling off these clothes right now, so we don't need no chair 'til we get through."

"Then I shall accept your hospitality." The doctor dropped heavily into the chair, evidence of an under-lying level of fatigue he was trying to conceal.

Without asking, Mary Jane brought him and James each a fresh cup of coffee.

"Thank you, young lady. I just finished an early morning delivery. Children are so inconsiderate as to the hours they choose to make their appearance.

Since you were looking for information in the newspaper, may I assume you know something of what
transpired yesterday?"

James nodded. "I did run afoul of something
going on last night. I stopped a white man from beating a black man, and he didn't take it too kindly."

"Ah? I'm sure he did not. I fear a lot of the feelings from the late military conflict still affects our
lives, and in a very significant way. I do know a bit
more about the event. I live over on South Street. I
was at home when I heard shots and, upon going to
the door, saw several policemen running up the
street, fleeing from a good-sized mob. When they
arrived at the bridge, one of those pursuing was shot,
I didn't see by whom. It seemed to end the mob's
interest in pursuit, but not the incident."

He took a sip of his coffee before he continued. "I
went to dress the wound, of course, and while I was
doing so, a large group of policemen arrived and
began firing on the colored people that had been in
the earlier group, doing so indiscriminately. I was
shocked to notice there were women and children in
their midst. It got very ugly. I tended a number of
wounds, and there were several dead. When I tended
some of the colored, some of the whites turned on
me, and the police had to intervene to save me."

James looked confused. "What brought it on? I've
never seen anything like it."

"As I understand it, there is a group of Negroes
called the Colored League. They recently procured a
fife and some drums and had been marching on the
outskirts of the town for several evenings. That

seemed to provoke the whites who thought it was a military demonstration and that they would eventually turn from marching to something violent."

"Why would anybody march around that didn't have to?"

The doctor continued to punctuate his sentences with sips from the cup. "This is excellent coffee," he told the ladies. "I've been thinking on that. I think for many of these colored men, being in the military was the first time they had ever been treated as somebody. I think it felt good for them to march together and more or less re-create the experience."

"It makes sense to me." They turned to see a newcomer standing at the edge of their camp. "I'm sorry. I didn't mean to be eavesdropping, but I overheard. I'm just a poor sharecropper, barely a step above them coloreds, and I understand why they'd march. I felt like a man while I was serving the Stars and Bars, at least until I got this." He pulled his hand out of his pocket to show that his right hand and arm were now useless.

James said, "Have a seat, Mr. ... ah ..."

"Johnson, Filbert Johnson." Mary Jane met him with a cup of coffee, and introductions went around again. He acknowledged them, then picked up his discourse. "I was fascinated to learn more about the riot last night. I've been wondering."

"Did you have some contact with it?" the doctor asked, studying Johnson's face.

"This morning. I was headed to Ryan's store when I saw a number of white men shoot and kill two colored soldiers. The soldiers just seemed to be walking along minding their own business. The group swelled into a mob that went over and set fire to the colored schoolhouse. They even started going into some of the homes of nearby coloreds and dragging out furniture to throw on the blaze. I never saw anything like it, and I saw some bad things while I was in the war. Terrible, just terrible."

"How awful," Mary Jane was captivated, not wanting to hear, but unable to keep from listening to the horrifying accounts. "What is the world coming to?"

Eleven

"Doc," James said, "I best bring Ma by your office tomorrow. I think she's ailing."

"Is that so? I see no reason to inconvenience her with such a trip unless it is absolutely necessary. Would you come and have a seat, Mrs. Campbell? I should be pleased to take a look at you." He removed his stethoscope from his bag.

Ma frowned, nervously wiping her hands on a towel. "There's no reason to make a fuss. I never had to see no doctor and don't see no reason to do so now."

"Now, Mrs. Campbell, if everyone felt that way I'd be out of business."

His charm was hard to resist. James gently

guided her to the chair, saying "I'd feel a sight better if you'd let him take a look, Ma. You know you ain't been yourself lately."

The doctor poked and prodded and listened through the stethoscope, but mostly he asked questions. "The shortness of breath began when you came down out of the mountains?"

"By the time I got to town. Always happens that way."

James agreed. "As we get down on the plains, it seems to get worse."

"Harder to get air in me down here," Ma said, convinced of the validity of her statement.

"Actually, it should be easier to breath the lower the altitude." The doctor replaced his equipment in his bag and took a seat again. "I've seen this before. I believe it to be a genuine medical malady, although I've not read of it in any medical journals and do not know if actually has a medical term or not. Have you ever met someone who could not stand to be shut up in a very tight place?"

James nodded. "Uncle Edgar was that way—he'd curl up and die if he was locked in the smokehouse."

"I think we've all met somebody like that, but may not be as aware that there are those who can't tolerate the exact opposite of that, public or very open places. I believe that to be at the root of your mother's problems. Mrs. Campbell, that is why it doesn't bother you as long as you are safely inside the wagon."

"Why am I just now coming down with it? I'm no spring chicken."

"Where did you live?"

"Up in the mountains."

"Closed in by trees and mountains?"

"Yes, most my life."

"There you have it; such an environment would be most suitable to a woman with this condition. It was the open spaces that started making you nervous, short of breath, not the change in altitude."

James frowned. "What can she do for it, Doctor?"

"Stay inside the wagon."

"Isn't there something you can give her for it?"

"I don't know what that'd be. It's going to get much worse as you get out on those wide-open plains."

Mary Jane didn't accept that. "Surely there has to be something we can do to help."

"Of course, now that you know what it is, use a windbreak when you set up camp—restrict that vision. I believe in time she may become accustomed to it once she knows what she's dealing with." He got up, put on his hat, and picked up his bag.

"What do I owe you, Doctor?"

"Not a thing, since there is really nothing I can directly do, we have done nothing more than discuss an interesting condition." He looked over at the pie cooling on the sideboard of the wagon. "Then again," he licked his lips, "a professional man is worthy of his hire. I would settle for a piece of that magnificent-looking pie."

Ma laughed. "I think you'll have to settle for the whole pie."

"I was going to take the ladies to town tomorrow,"

James had a worried look on his face, "but now I don't know if that's a good idea."

"I think it's safe to do so. Mrs. Campbell, you have a large, full bonnet, do you not?"

"You're talking about putting blinders on me like a horse?"

He laughed. "I would have not put it so indelicately, but I think it would help. If you get too uncomfortable, just return to the wagon."

The following morning, James took them to Ryan's store to shop. In spite of the doctor's assurance that it was safe, he stood outside on the sidewalk as Ma and Mary Jane went in to shop.

They had found a number of the items on their list when Ma spotted the ripe tomatoes. "We'll just get a couple of these for while we are here. They wouldn't last any length of time on the trail."

The storekeeper smiled. "I can help you with that. If you'll take these tomatoes and scald them in the usual way, then strip off the skins and mash them through a sieve, it'll produce an even pulp. Stew that pulp slowly, to get rid of as much water as possible—but without burning—then spread it in the sun on plates or in a slow oven."

"It'll dry up."

"Yes'm, then when you want to use it, you only have to take out a portion, soak it and cook it a few minutes, and serve it up just as you would tomatoes stewed fresh from the garden."

"Can you imagine? Does that really work?"

"Absolutely, and if you have a few of these airtights, it'll help keep the tomatoes fresh even longer."

"Never seen one; what's it do?" She picked up the glass container. It had a handle on it something like the handle on a milk pail; only it was crooked and snapped into place to exert a strong pressure on the lid that fit the jar.

"The jar will seal when this handle is snapped in place," he demonstrated. "It shuts out air and keeps things fresh longer. If you heat these jars in a pan of water before you do this, it'll develop a vacuum as it cools, and that really seals them tight."

"What a wonder. How much are they?"

"Thirty cents a dozen. They really will pay for themselves in the long run."

"James don't leave much in the way of leftovers to save, but if they'd help us hang onto fresh food longer, I reckon that really would save money."

"That tomato idea really would help a trail stew, wouldn't it?" Mary Jane said. "Why don't we get the jars and store up some tomatoes like he says?"

"I guess it'd be a good idea."

As the storekeeper added the jars to their order, Mary Jane moved down the counter. "Oh, look at this, Ma. Isn't it beautiful?"

The storekeeper put on his salesman's smile. "That's the most popular bonnet in Paris this season, miss." He pulled out a piece of paper. "This ad they gave us says to notice that the sides sit closely to the face, and the front is heart shaped, drooping slightly at the extreme edge toward the forehead. The crowns are made round and firm, and it comes in gray and purple, and in café au lait and silver." He set the ad aside. "It's the very latest thing."

She put it back wistfully. "*A dollar eighty?* I can't afford it. They must think it's made of solid gold."

Ma smiled. "If you're going to set your bonnet for Ross, it should be a really *nice* bonnet."

"Do you think ...?"

"I do." They added it to the order.

"I think I'll wear it now."

The shopkeeper smiled. "There's a mirror right over there."

Mary Jane walked around the edge of the counter to face the mirror, stubbing her toe on a brass spittoon set just around the corner. "Well, my goodness." She bent down to move it out of her way. "They should be careful where they set these things."

She looked into the mirror and tied the strings of the bonnet. The results were quite pleasing. "It looks so good on you," Ma said.

"We'll send your order to the wagon yard in a buggy so you won't have to carry it," the shopkeeper said pleasantly.

"How nice." They gave him a bright smile as he held the door for them to leave.

Behind the storekeeper, the clerk headed to the window to set up a display of newly shipped canned peaches. The last thing he expected was for the spittoon to be sitting in the middle of the aisle behind the counter. He tripped over it. With the canned peaches in his arms, he couldn't check his momentum and began to fall forward in a stumbling run. "Oh nooooooo!"

The shopkeeper looked over his shoulder in time to see the young man, and an armload of items intended for display, go crashing through the front window. The young man landed at Mary Jane's feet.

"Well, my goodness."

"Pardon, miss," he said as he reached to tip his hat, only to discover it was no longer on his head. It confused him. "Hope you aren't hurt."

Mary Jane and Ma helped him to his feet. "Not at all, but are you all right?"

The clerk looked at the furious face of his boss. "For the time being."

James came walking up. "What happened?"

"This young man seems to have had a mishap," Ma explained.

"You don't say. Well, I came to fetch and carry."

"The shopkeeper said they'd send our order in a buggy."

"They're gonna tote it for us? Imagine that."

He extended his arms to the two ladies, and they each took an elbow. "Mighty pretty bonnet, Mary Jane."

Her face lit up. "You think so?"

"I do."

"You think Ross will like it?"

"Hummmph."

"I beg your pardon?"

As they turned to go back to their camp, a booming voice behind them called out, "Steamboat a-coming!" They looked back at the source of the call, an old black man, cupping his hand as he repeated the call several times in a resounding baritone voice. The town that had been quiet and composed came alive. The trio found themselves caught up in the flow toward the wharves. Drays and carts began to clatter by, stores closed, young girls and boys magically appeared.

People gathered on the levee, pointing to a plume of black smoke coming from two stacks. "It's the *Cheyenne*," a nearby man announced knowledgeably. "That's Captain Kyle's packet. She's right on time."

"A riverboat?" Ma said. "How exciting. I never imagined there was a river big enough for such a thing, but now that I see it, it's huge. How will we ever ford that?" She began to twist the handkerchief held in her hands, and her breath began to come in short gasps.

The knowledgeable man said, "There's no fording the Mighty Mississippi, ma'am. Why, she can get as deep as eighty feet."

She wasn't listening any longer. Mary Jane turned her away from the river.

"How do we get a wagon across?" James asked.

"You'll need to take the ferry. It carries freight and wagons and such. Go see Josiah over there, the man with the red beard and faded pilot's hat. He can answer your questions. I'd do it before the boat docks though."

James went over as the man suggested.

"Oh, look there," Mary Jane gasped. "It's beautiful!" The *Cheyenne* was in view now. It stood tall above the water, glass pilothouse some thirty feet above the Texas deck. Passengers lined the lower deck, their first view of Memphis as enticing to them as the view of the vessel was to the townsfolk.

The sound of the ship's bell rolled across the water, and the steam whistle seemed to shake the earth with its giant bellow. Deckhands scurried with ropes, matched by a corresponding effort on the dock. It all seemed choreographed.

The captain shouted an order, a bell rang, and the giant stern wheel stopped. The craft was white with gingerbread trim and gilt touches here and there. Ropes were tossed and secured. A large gangplank was lowered into place, and passengers and freight began to come and go. Blacks and whites scurried here and there, taking no notice of one another, the difficulties of the last couple of days seemingly forgotten.

The dock was like an anthill that had been stirred by a stick. The activity lasted some fifteen or twenty minutes, then with cries of "All ashore that's going ashore," accompanied by the bellowing whistle, the riverboat backed out and continued its journey.

"All that excitement for a boat?" Ma said.

"It was magical," Mary Jane answered. "Bigger than life. I felt a pull, as if it was beckoning me to come on board, promising that some great adventure awaited me out there somewhere."

Ma scowled, "Hummmph, I've already got all the great adventure that I can handle, thank you. I can't stand so many people."

James returned from talking with the river pilot. "He told me everything I need to know. We're going to Arkansas tomorrow."

Ma looked out over the water. The color seemed to have drained out of her face. Her fear of the open space was replaced by a new worry. "I can't swim. I'm going to sink into that river tomorrow and drown, I just know it."

James hugged her with a strong right arm. "Oh, don't be silly, Ma. We won't let you drown. Let's get you back to the wagon, I think you've seen enough for one day."

Slim strode through the door into Osborne's place. His face was black with soot. He stepped up to the bar, and Osborne poured him a drink. "Somebody else is gonna have to light the fire next time," he observed to nobody in particular. "I got my tailfeathers scorched good."

"We'd best get it done then while they're occupied," said Scott. "This here is Ross."

"Ross, eh? Bet Osborne could blow out a candle on that one."

Osborne made a face at him, and they filed out.

As they crossed the imaginary line separating No Man's Land from the Texas border, they could see black smoke off in the distance. Cattle milled around, seemingly unprotected. They reined in on the other side, and Scott said to Ross, "You wear those Colts just for show?"

"I can use 'em."

"All right, we'll start loose-herding a few of these critters across the Red. You ride back over and keep an eye on the XIT crew. We'll need a four-hour lead. If they come after us before then, you fall back and make it unprofitable for them to come ahead."

"I can do that."

They rode toward the herd, and Ross yelled, "Scott!"

The outlaw pulled up and looked back. "Yeah?"

"If you get any ideas about running off so you don't have to split, just remember that cows ain't all that hard to track."

"Never entered my head."

James and the ladies left camp at first light after a cold breakfast in an attempt to be first at the ferry, but as soon as they got a view of the river, they were shocked to see lines of vehicles waiting their turn on both sides, going and coming. Shuffling back and forth was a splendid steam ferryboat, the *Miss Ella*. The river was about three-fourths of a mile wide, and the ferry could transport about fifteen to twenty wagons and teams at a time. It was rainy and cold, and the captain was letting the females from the wagons board and wait in the ferry sitting room, until their wagons were delivered across.

The river was a wonder. There were lumber rafts and coal barges floating by, so low in the water that the men walking on them appeared to be treading on the water. Little trading scows plied their trade, calling on farms and plantations up and down the river. Several keelboats made their way past, hugging the shoreline so the poles could touch ground as the rows of men walked down each side to push against the muddy river bottom. As they ran out of boat, the men raised the poles, walked inside the line of men coming toward them, and took their place again at the rear.

"I can see that that would work pretty well going downriver," James said, "but it looks like it'd be mighty tough coming back upstream."

"Oh, they don't come back," a man explained. "They sell the boat in New Orleans, ride a steamboat back upriver, build a new one, and start over."

An old man was selling fish over on the bank. He had a wagon full, catfish freshly caught, and people were gathered around his astonishing display. One fish was said to weigh close to three hundred pounds. James bought a smaller one for twenty cents. It weighed only twenty pounds and looked like a minnow next to the huge monster in the wagon.

It was noon before James loaded the wagon and prepared to cross. He found the ladies and escorted them back to the wagon to disembark. He opened the paper to show them the fish he had bought for supper. As soon as the huge head and glaring eye was uncovered, Mary Jane jerked back. "Oh my."

When she recoiled, the tip of her umbrella caught a crewman in the lower back, prodding him forward. He fought for balance, teeter-tottering on the rail, before he lost the battle and disappeared over the side in a hail of most nautical but quite unseemly language.

From the deckhouse, the cry "Man overboard!" was sounded, bells rang, the whistle blew, the engine stopped, and fellow crewmen scurried to effect a rescue.

"What do you suppose that is all about?" James asked as he looked over the side at the man flailing in the water, angrily shaking his fist.

"I don't know," Mary Jane sniffed. "But as that fellow jumped over the side, he let go with the most uncouth language."

Ma nodded knowingly. "Probably having family troubles. All he's going to accomplish is just getting wet and more miserable. These fellers are not going to let him drown himself."

"Well, let's get loaded up," said James. "We'll want to get this guy on a spit over the fire while he's still fresh. He's so big, I expect we can fillet him and cook him like steaks."

Mary Jane looked horrified. "*What?*"

James laughed. "I was talking about the fish, not the man in the water."

Twelve

*S*locum couldn't resist riding to the black smoke on the horizon. As he approached, he saw the foreman sitting off to the side, yelling orders. He rode over to him. "You the foreman? Can I help out?"

"Ranger, good to see you. Reckon we can use all the help we can get. We've got all the fire drags that we have in use. The boys are starting to cut some steers in half to use them for drags."

"That's pretty drastic," responded Slocum.

"You use what you've got."

"Bet the boss man hates that."

"He'd be hot were he here, all right. Cut you a horse out of the remuda if you want to help, riding that fire line is hard on them. Change mounts real often too; we don't want to ruin good horses."

Slocum cut out a horse, saddled it, and rode over to the fire line. He threw a rope on one of the carcasses and started riding along the fire line, dragging the beef right down the edge of the flames. "We fighting fire or having a barbecue?" he yelled.

"You like your beef well done, you can have it when we're through," a cowboy yelled back. "You'd better get that bandanna pulled up; it don't take long to get your nose clogged out here."

Up on the ridgeline Ross watched the activity with interest. He couldn't believe the rustlers had caused all of this mess just to distract the ranch hands long enough for them to steal a few cows. Away from the scene of the main battle, he saw several cowboys with teams and plows making a firebreak between the flames and the house. If they got the flames down a bit before the fire got there, it wouldn't be able to jump the break.

Ross stayed there, watching for a couple of hours. The house was safe, and the cowhands were trying to knock down a few hot spots. Nobody was showing any signs of leaving. He eased down from the ridge, mounted, and headed back to town.

Down below, Slocum stopped and looked around him. He had a sudden premonition that Campbell was around, but he didn't see anything. *I'd better not find out he had anything to do with this fire.*

As James and the ladies moved away from the river, the terrain became a mixture of swamps and prairies in the expansive Delta region of eastern

Arkansas. For a distance of 150 miles, the table-flat landscape was broken only once by a narrow ridge hardly a mile wide and a hundred feet high that ran from north to south across their path. Provisions were easier to obtain with an abundance of ducks, turkeys, prairie chickens, quail, and the occasional deer and bear. James never set his cap for a bear, as that was more meat than they could handle on the trail. November was upon them, and the roads were getting muddier, slowing their progress. The ladies were riding rather than slogging through the mud on foot, but then Ma was more comfortable within the confines of the wagon anyway.

Ma glanced up from her knitting. Her chair rocked of its own accord with the motion of the wagon. "You've been reading in that Bible a lot— coming up with any answers?"

Mary Jane frowned at the Bible, closed it, and held it up. "More questions than answers."

"Bible study can be like that. Any time you want to talk, I'm ready. I figure the most useless thing in the world is unwanted advice though, so I don't go offering any unless I'm asked."

Mary Jane moved over to sit beside the rocker. She handled the swaying of the wagon as an old sailor handled the moving deck on a ship. "I still get this uneasy feeling every time I read. I don't understand. You and James read it, and it brings you a sense of peace. I can see that it comforts you. Why doesn't it comfort me?"

"Much of what is in there is beyond our understanding until we have the Holy Spirit in us, helping us to get it."

"Then I guess I'm not getting that help."

"God is still dealing with you. I don't know what about; it's a very personal thing. Are you sure you're on the road to heaven?"

"I can't say. You and James seem so sure you are heaven bound. I just hope I am. I hope I've lived a good 'nuff life."

"How you live ain't what saves you, girl. We can't earn our way into heaven. It's a gift. Jesus died for us to save us from our sins. All He asks is that we believe in Him and confess Him as our Savior and Lord. 'Course, we're supposed to live the best we can after we become one of His flock, but it ain't the works that gets us in; it's our faith in Him and His love and grace."

"Maybe that's it. I don't think I've ever been saved, at least not in the way you describe it. Some of what the Bible is talking about is starting to make sense to me though."

"You stay after it. It's the most important thing you'll ever do."

Ross caught up with the rustlers and helped them finish the drive; then they split up the money from the sale. It was easy money, but now that he knew Slocum was in the neighborhood he didn't plan on waiting around for him to show up.

He rode away toward the eastern part of Indian Territory, to the lands of the civilized tribes, particularly the Cherokee, who lived in towns and farmed and generally fared better than most whites out in No Man's Land.

As he traveled along, Ross noticed with great appreciation the towns and buildings of the tribes. They made the Campbell place back in the Cumberland Mountains look like what it was, a hard-scrabble, dirt-poor farm. He rode into a little town named Sudden.

It was big enough to have a hotel and a saloon. He could hear the chips clinking on the poker table, his kind of town. He boarded his horse, got a room and a bath, and looked to find some action.

Maybe I'll keep going east over into Arkansas; see how far that ranger will chase me. I might even go on home and see Ma. That'd be kinda nice. And that little gal back there, what was her name?

At Little Rock, in the center of the state, the terrain had begun to change from swamps and prairies to gradually ascending hills and valleys as the trio made their way upland toward Fort Smith, some 160 miles away. When they arrived and then pushed on west, the Arkansas River that divided Arkansas from Indian Territory was a snap after having crossed the Mississippi. The trio went over on a small ferry poled across by several deckhands. One of them again ended up in the water, though no one seemed to quite know how or why. Mary Jane pointed out that it seemed to be a common occurrence in their profession and always seemed to produce the same behavior.

The travelers hadn't been in the Territory long when they were stopped, and a voice said, "Get those hands up, Campbell."

James complied. "How'd you know my name?"

"Name, face, habits," said Slocum. "I've been trailing you for months."

Ma stuck her head through the canvas at the front of the wagon. "From Tennessee?"

Slocum removed his hat. "Howdy, ma'am. No, from down Texas way. I'm a Texas Ranger." He pinned on his badge.

"That's silly." Slocum turned to see who was speaking behind him and spied Mary Jane coming up from the rear of the wagon. "We've never even been to Texas."

"I don't know about you, miss, but Campbell sure has—I've seen him." He pointed at James with his pistol.

"I think I see the problem here," Ma said as she moved up beside James on the seat. "When you saw him, was he dressed like this?"

"No, ma'am, that farmer's getup is a right fine disguise, but I recognized him right off."

"Mr. Slocum, was it?"

"Yes, ma'am."

"Mr. Slocum, may I present you to my son James Campbell? I suspect you may have already made the acquaintance of his twin brother, Ross."

"*Twins?* Are you funning me, ma'am?" He slipped his Colt back into the holster and crossed his arms on his saddle horn.

"Not a bit."

"Well, if that don't beat all."

Thirteen

*S*locum eased into the saloon, stepping immediately to the side to put the wall to his back as he surveyed the room. He spotted Ross at a table on the other side of the room. There were two other card games in progress, three men standing at the bar, and one guy singing off-key songs as he tried to play on the out-of-tune piano. Slocum cataloged the faces, decided there was no imminent danger, and moved to the end of the bar.

"Campbell," he said loudly, "I've come a long way looking for you."

The table and the bar between the two men cleared as if by magic.

Ross threw his cards into the middle of the table

with disgust. "First good hand I've had all evening. You gotta be Slocum."

"That's right."

"That ranger badge don't cut no ice over here."

"I'm getting really tired of hearing that. Anyway, I'm figuring you're gonna volunteer to come back with me."

Ross pushed his hat back on his head with his left hand, keeping his right near his gun. They were so focused on each other, they didn't notice James and Mary Jane enter the door. She started to call out to Ross, but James put his hand on her arm to silence her, then moved her out of the line of fire against the bar.

"I don't feel much like volunteering," Ross said. *You ain't left me no play, Slocum,* he thought. *If you'd jumped me on the trail, I mighta gone with you and taken my chances on getting away. But I ain't got it in me to back down in front of all these guys.*

Slocum thumbed the strap off the hammer of his pistol. His eyes were cold and deadly. "Don't make me carry you back over a saddle."

Mary Jane realized what was about to happen. Her hand went to her mouth, and her eyes got as wide as silver dollars. With the movement of her hand, her elbow caught an empty beer mug on the bar and sent it spinning to the floor.

The sudden crash made Slocum turn and draw. He saw no danger and spun back to Ross ... too late. He almost got off a shot before Ross fired, the slug smashing into his shoulder, half-turning him to the bar. It took a precious second, maybe two, to absorb the shock, shift his Walker Colt to his left hand, then turn to continue making his play ... again too late.

With quick steps Ross closed the gap, knocked the gun from Slocum's hand, then drew a bead right on the ranger's forehead. "I can't abide this constant chasing, Slocum. Reckon if I don't do for you, one of these other boys will." He ratcheted back the hammer.

"Ross Allen Campbell!" He flinched, easing back on the hammer. Men never get too old to flinch when their mother uses their full name on them.

He kept the ranger covered as he glanced over toward her. "Ma? What are you doing here?"

"I'm looking for you."

"Ain't that sweet?" a hard case by the wall ventured. "Mama's come for her baby boy."

Ross spun on him, his eyes hard and flat. "You want to buy into this game?"

"Shut up, Sanders," someone said. "Reckon most of us would still mind our ma if'n she was to come in on us."

Sanders made a wry face. "You just go get your ma out of here. We'll take care of Slocum for you."

James had ducked out the door when the action started. He came back in with a double-barrel shotgun, jerked back the hammers, and said, "Nobody is doing anything with this man. You know what this scattergun will do at this range. Mister, you'd best come with me."

"I'll be taking my pistol," Slocum said, holding out his left hand to Ross.

"You must think I'm fat between the ears."

He kept the hand extended. "Nobody carries Walker Colts but Texas Rangers, and a few army officers. I'm not letting it get away from me."

"I kinda fancy it myself."

"I'm not leaving without it."

"Oh, good grief, give it to *me*." Ma stalked over to jerk the weapon out of Ross's hand. "Now you come with me, both of you."

A big bearded man by the door said, "You mind your mother before I fetch you a lick up beside the head."

There was no recovering his pride now. Ross just holstered his pistol and started for the door. Mary Jane could stand it no longer. She ran the few steps separating them to throw her arms around his neck. "Oh, Ross, Ross, I thought I'd never see you again."

"What the ... oh, I get it." He searched his memory, but no name would come forth. "So it's you. Now it makes sense. I figured I was done for. I knew I couldn't take that ranger." He swung her around and around as she clung to his neck. "For once your little 'accidents' worked to somebody's disadvantage besides mine. Reckon you saved my bacon for sure."

"Me? I didn't do anything."

"I know, darlin'. You never do."

The big man watched them leave, then in a loud voice aimed at no one in particular, announced, "I won't tolerate anybody making a play for that ranger around those nice ladies."

"Ah, nothing good ever come out of shootin' no

lawman anyway," said Sanders. "Stirs the rest of 'em up like a hornet's nest."

The Campbell party bedded Slocum down in the back of the wagon, and the women tended his wounds as James put some miles between them and the little town. If they had been out in No Man's Land when the confrontation occurred, chances are no amount of intervention would have saved the lawman. Indian Territory wasn't as wild as No Man's Land, but still no real law prevailed there.

Ross rode beside the wagon. He knew the ranger wouldn't give up the chase. His thoughts were focused on the only way he knew to have any peace. His twin knew him too well, however, and James looked over to where his brother rode in silence. "If you're still thinking you should have finished off Slocum, you know we ain't going to let you do it."

Ross grinned. "You thinking you'll stop me? You ain't never been able to stop me from anything I ever wanted to do."

James motioned with his head, saying, "That's only because of those guns. Man-to-man I can take you every time, and you know it. If you'd taken your turns behind the plow, you might have enough muscle to get it done, but you didn't."

Ross found that remark funny. "Most of your muscle is in your head trying to scratch a living out of that dirt farm. I take it you finally had to toss in your hand?"

"The bank took it. You never sent any money like

you said you were going to."

"To help keep a dead farm alive? If a farm can't be a paying proposition without pumping money into it from the outside, it don't deserve to make it."

"It don't matter to you that Ma lost her home?"

Ross frowned. "I feel bad about losing the home place. Just knowing it was there was the only kind of roots I had. Kinda works on me knowing it's gone. You got money now?"

James shook his head. "Not much. We'd have run out a long time ago, but Mary Jane fed money into the pot." He didn't want to admit they had only made it this far because he had taken money from a girl.

He shouldn't have worried—that wasn't what Ross was thinking at all. *Mary Jane, that's it. I was wanting to find out what to call her without anybody discovering I didn't remember her name.* "Well, I'm pretty flush, so I can give you a couple hundred dollars."

"*A couple hundred!* Are you kidding me? I never saw a hundred dollars at one time in my whole life."

"I know, plowboy. Why do you think I left? I'm not geared to scratch at the dirt for peanuts."

"Where'd you get this money? Is it dirty?" James knew his brother only too well.

"All money is dirty. Handled by who knows how many people, and a lot of them doing things I don't even want to think about before they handled it. I'd say slopping pigs is cleaner work than handling money."

"That's not what I'm asking, and you know it."

"I figure you know better than to ask a question like that."

"That's what I was afraid of."

"Oh, don't get so high and mighty on me. I won it at cards; that shouldn't soil your delicate sensibilities."

James glared at his twin. "I don't hold with gambling either, but I reckon for Ma's sake I ought to shut up and take it."

Ross smirked. "Sounds to me like you're still keeping your head stuck in that Bible all the time."

"You know I am. You could stand to read it more yourself."

"Bunch of superstitious claptrap. I can't believe you buy into all that stuff."

"I can't believe you don't."

Ross shook his head. "Same old argument." He pulled up his collar; the wind was coming up, sharp and strong.

"Nothing ever changes."

"Here you are homeless, living in a wagon, toting around an old woman and a jonah of a girl, and you say nothing ever changes?"

"What do you mean 'a jonah of a girl'?"

Ross laughed. "Are you telling me you haven't had any bad luck since Mary Jane started traveling with you?"

"We were having a run of bad luck before she started traveling with us. We lost the farm, remember?"

"But other stuff started happening, right? An accident here and there?"

"There have been a few accidents, all right, but she didn't have anything to do with them."

"Oh yeah, right." He rode over close to the wagon and handed James some folded bills. "You tuck this money into your overalls, and keep it to yourself."

James took it without a word.

"Since you three seem to be determined to stand between me and that ranger, I guess I don't have it in me to finish him off if'n I have to hurt you to do it. It'll take you a while to nurse him back to health, so I should get a good lead that way."

"You're leaving?"

"I've got to."

"Aren't you going to say good-bye? You know we came out here hunting you. Ma ain't going to give up, and neither is Mary Jane."

Ross looked surprised. "She came out here hunting me? I thought she was here with you."

"She doesn't have feelings for me; it's you she wants."

Ross shook his head vigorously. "Then I'm sure not saying good-bye to either of them before I leave. I have enough bad luck without tying myself to it. Where'd she get the idea I wanted her with me?"

"From things you said."

"I never pledged myself to her, just said a few sweet things trying to bed her, without success, I might add. Every time I'd get close, that curse of hers would kick in, and some calamity would come roaring down on me like my hair catching on fire or some of that other stuff."

"Oh, I gotta hear that one."

"Too long a story, and I don't like to think about

it. Besides, I gotta get gone. You tell her I don't want her tagging along with me."

It was James's turn to shake his head vigorously. "You tell her yourself. She won't believe me."

"Not on your life. If she can make all these things happen by accident, I'd hate to think what she might do on purpose if she was mad at me." He swung his horse. "Tell Ma I said good-bye."

Fourteen

*I*t made Ma mad. "That boy! Here I come all this way looking for him, and he don't even stay around long enough to say howdy. I won't stand for it. We got to go catch up to him."

Mary Jane sobbed deeply. "He didn't want me to come with him?"

James wasn't taking the blame. "I told him to at least say good-bye, but he told me to do it for him." He looked at the ranger. "And you know we can't go after him, not yet."

Mary Jane wasn't letting him off the hook. "James, you're ignoring me."

James threw down his hat. It wasn't fair for Ross to put him in this position. "I didn't want to be the one to have to tell you. I told him he should do it himself."

Mary Jane's eyes were blazing. She put her hands on her hips. "Tell me what?"

There was no escaping it. He might as well get it over with. "Tell you that you don't mean anything to him. No, more than that, I might as well get it said. He thinks you're a jinx, Mary Jane, bad luck."

She lifted her hands in resignation and looked toward the sky. "Where do men get that? I've been hearing it for years. He said I was nothing to him? Nothing at all?"

How far was he going to have to take this? "I'm sorry, Mary Jane. It looks like the feelings between you were always one sided."

She began to sob again. The ranger's eyes opened slowly. He had passed out when they had probed to make sure the bullet had gone clear through. While he was out, they had cleaned and dressed the wound best as they could with what little they had in the wagon.

"How long have I been out?" Slocum demanded.

"An hour, give or take," Ma said.

He looked at James. "Your brother?"

"He tore outta here like his pants was afire. Got a few miles behind him by now."

Slocum looked over at Mary Jane. She had her back turned, but her shoulders were heaving. "That why this little lady is cryin'?"

"It is."

"Trust me, it's for the best." He looked at Mary Jane. "Miss, you deserve better than the likes of him." Slocum tried to sit up, but the pain stopped him.

Ma put a hand on him to restrain him. "It'll be a couple of days before you can get up, if you don't want to open that wound back up. And a few more after that before you can ride."

Slocum was upset. "He's getting away."

Ma shook her head. "He ain't. My boy James thinks with the same head. He don't have to track him—he can *feel* where he's going."

Slocum didn't understand that type of thinking at all. "You got to pardon me, ma'am, but why should I believe you'd help me? I'm going to be taking your son back to face justice."

"We're plain folk, Mr. Slocum. If my boy done bad, I want him to face up to it and set things right."

Slocum looked at James. "That go for you too?" He didn't understand these people.

"It does. Ma raised us to clean up our own messes. It's time Ross was made to clean up his."

Ross tried to figure out where he stood. *How long can they keep that ranger flat on his back—three, maybe four days? Then he'll be coming after me. If I head to Mexico, will he cross the border? He came into the Territory after me. Be an awful long ride to the border if I don't go through Texas.*

He thought he had it figured right. He would have to chance it, win, lose, or draw. He would ride through Texas and on down across the border. Surely no one would expect him to do that.

Slocum managed to get his pants on over his long johns, but there was no way to pull his boots on. Not the way Ma had had James snub his left arm tight against his chest to keep him immobilized. Slocum put his good arm in a shirtsleeve, pulled it taut, and buttoned it. *Under the circumstances, reckon that's as presentable as I'm gonna get.*

He scooted out on the tailgate and eased himself to the ground. Even taking all the care he could, the impact brought an "ummpph" from him. Hearing it, Ma descended on him like a duck on a June bug.

"Mr. Slocum, you shouldn't be up." She pinned him up against the wagon, jerking open his shirt and the top of his long johns to inspect his shoulder.

"Ma'am ... ma'am ... *ma'am!*"

"Quit your caterwauling. Well, looks like you haven't busted anything loose." She pulled the garments back into place, buttoned him back up, and pointed to the rocking chair by the fire. "Sit yourself down—breakfast is almost ready."

"No, ma'am. It come to me when I woke up this morning that I did you ladies out of your bed. I'm not going to add to that by taking your rocking chair. I'll just sit over on that stump." Barefoot, he began to pick his way toward the stump.

Ma walked over to the chuck box and pulled out a rolling pin. "Mr. Slocum, if you want me to take your mind off the pain in your shoulder, you're going about it in the right manner. While you are under my care, you had best learn to mind or suffer the consequences."

"Yes, ma'am." He hobbled over to the chair and sat, immediately receiving a cup of hot coffee from Mary Jane. She was humming a pleasant little tune.

"You seem to be in better spirits this morning, miss."

She smiled. "I have decided Ross said all those terrible things because he knew he couldn't take me with him, so he was trying to spare my feelings. I am undeterred. I shall track him down and have him explain it to my face. Oh my, you're buttoned crooked." Before he could object, she quickly unbuttoned and rebuttoned his shirt, then went about her work, resuming her humming.

"Come and get it!" Ma shouted to James. Slocum got up to go as well, but Mary Jane had buttoned the last rung of the chair arm inside his shirt. As it came tight, it threw him off balance, yanking him back into the chair and upending the coffee in his lap.

"Hot ... hot ... oh ... hot!"

James saw his predicament and threw a dipper of water at the ranger's lap. "Thankya, James, wet is better than scalded." He looked toward the ladies and shook his head. "A man never knows how much he needs some good old-fashioned cusswords to get him through a tough situation until they're taken from him."

"What happened?"

"I have no idea."

Ross was starting to second-guess his sanity. *Whatever possessed me to give James two hundred dollars? That's better'n half of everything I had. Showing off, I guess. Maybe I was taking care of Ma; reckon I owed it to her.*

He thought the look on James's face had been worth it though. What if somebody had done that to his daddy, who'd been dirt poor all his life? That was something he would like to have been able to see.

His mind returned to Mary Jane. He couldn't believe she had believed all the malarkey he had fed her back in the mountains. She had believed it so much she had come running right after him. He had always figured that no man in his right mind would team up with a filly like that, what with misfortune following her like a black cloud. *I don't figure on being that close to her, not ever again.*

Ross topped the hill. Down at the bottom, a man wearing blue pants and a white shirt was standing out in a stream. A young lady in a white cotton dress stood by him. He was speaking in a loud voice that carried to Ross, although he couldn't make out the words. After the loud words, the man suddenly turned, grabbed the girl, and held her under the water.

Ross's hand went to his gun, and he spurred his horse, but before the animal got up any speed, the man pulled the girl back up. It was only then that Ross noticed a crowd on the opposite hill begin to hoot and holler. Ross reined in his horse and took his hand off his pistol. *It's that traveling preacher. I can't believe I've run afoul of him again.* He rode on down.

"Well, if it isn't Ross Campbell," Amos said warmly. "Good to see you again. Come share the Word of the Lord with us."

"Thanks, Preacher, but I reckon I've got all the religion I can use. Where'd these people come from? Is there a town near here?"

"None of us has all the religion we can use. The

more we get, the more we need, so it sounds to me like you don't have much."

Ross stopped on the bank overlooking the man. "No offense, Parson, but I wish you'd lay off that stuff."

"I know how you feel. I've been where you are now and not so long ago."

"You didn't answer me about the town."

"These people came from farms and ranches, near and far. The word spread, and they came. There's no town near here that I know of."

"Ain't that water cold?"

"It is most assuredly cold, bordering on freezing, but it is surely worth it, considering what we're doing."

"What you're doing is standing in freezing water up to your waist, arguing with me. If I were you, I'd get into some dry clothes and do your preaching to those folks sitting there waiting to hear it."

Ross reined his horse around. "I've got family following a couple of days behind me. My brother loves this stuff, and so does my ma. She's with him. If you're still here, that is."

"God stopped me here, Ross. He tells me when to go and when to stop—and I gotta tell ya, whatever He brought me here for hasn't happened yet, but I'll know it when it does. We've had several folks get saved, some get married, and some just figured it was time to get right with God."

"You have an appointment coming, all right. There's a lady on her way that'll test that religion of yours." Ross rode away, laughing to himself.

Fifteen

Slocum hobbled to the fire where James was reading aloud from the Bible. "You're welcome to join us," James said. "We read from the Bible each night."

"Can't go wrong with that." He lowered himself into position on the stump.

"Are you a child of the King?" Ma asked kindly.

Slocum rubbed his shoulder and worked his arm gingerly. "My own mama helped me get my name written in the Lamb's Book of Life many years ago. I reckon my profession and lifestyle may cause me to have a little explaining to do at the judgment seat, but it's a comfort knowing I'm saved in spite of all that."

"Are you saying you believe you're saved even though you know you've done things that were wrong?" Mary Jane asked.

"You'll have to forgive Mary Jane for being so forward with her questions," Ma explained to the lawman. "She's wrestling with her own religious standing right now."

Slocum looked serious. "Miss Mary Jane, I ain't got a preaching bone in my body, and that's a fact, but I know our eternal destiny is something we oughta get settled as soon as possible. Out in this wild country, there's a hundred things that could happen to us before the sun comes up tomorrow. It just don't pay to tarry."

The Campbell party topped the hill to see the crowd again assembled to hear the preacher in the valley. The noise of the wagon coming down the hill drew everyone's attention. They stopped and watched as it pulled up on the bank of the stream.

Amos walked over to welcome the new arrivals. "I'm Brother Amos. You've just about missed the doings here. I figure to head out in the morning, but better late than never." He looked closely at them. Something registered with him, he wasn't sure what, but he knew what it meant. "I feel sure God sent me here for a reason, and all of a sudden I think that reason is one of you. I'm pretty sure you can tell me who it is."

Those in the wagon held their peace. They knew it was up to Mary Jane to speak up.

Amos saw that he would have to approach them

differently. "It's hard, isn't it? Lemme put it this way: Do all of you here have your names in the Lamb's Book of Life?"

There was a quick murmured assent ... from all but one. Amos held out his hand to Mary Jane. "I'm sorry to single you out that way, but it looks like I'm here for you." He helped her down from the wagon. "Don't worry, I'm not figuring on putting a bunch of pressure on you. God doesn't work that way, and neither do I. I can see you don't want to talk in front of all these people."

He turned and spoke to the group behind him. "Brother Joseph, some singing is in order. Would you see what you can accomplish? How about you folks in the wagon getting down and joining them?"

A couple of youngsters started pumping the organ in the back of the wagon, and Judy began the strains of "Rock of Ages." Soon Joseph's clear baritone led those assembled in the familiar old hymn.

James and Ma helped Slocum down and went to join the group while Amos and Mary Jane walked farther down the creek. When they got a short distance away from the others, he stopped and simply waited for her to talk.

She spoke very quietly, and he had to strain to hear. "I don't know whether I'm saved or not. I've been talking to Ma and reading the Bible and trying to understand what it means, but I'm finding it all very confusing."

"It was hard to me, too, really hard," said Amos. "I didn't want to believe any of it. Sounds like you're further along than I was. At least you aren't fighting it."

She spun to face him. "They tell me the first step is admitting that I'm a sinner, but I'm not. I live a good life; I never use profanity, lie, or steal."

He smiled. "I know what you're trying to say, but none of us are without sin, even after we become children of God. Believe me, there has only been One who was perfect: Jesus Christ. That's why only the sinless Son of God could be the sacrifice for our sin. You say you've been reading the Bible. Did you see where it says that since the beginning of time a blood sacrifice has always been required for the remission of sin?"

"Yes, I've read that."

"Do you believe that Jesus shed His blood on the cross so that the sins of the whole world could be washed away and that sinners could be saved?"

"Yes, I believe that."

Amos took hold of both her hands. "Then, you're already where you need to be. You have all of the pieces right in your hands. You just need to put them together. You need to admit to God that you are a sinner; that you know that Jesus died to save you, and that you claim the gift of redemption He offers you. You don't have a problem with any of that, do you?"

"No, not really. I guess I am a sinner if you put it that way, and I sure enough believe in what He has done for me, for us all."

"Then let's pray together." They knelt together as she prayed and accepted the sacrifice of Jesus for her sins and put her faith and trust in Him to save her. As they walked back to where the people were gathered, Amos said, "If you're ready, I'll baptize you. I've been doing a lot of that the last couple of days."

She nodded her head, and together they walked into the stream. The water was terribly cold, but neither of them seemed to notice. He looked up at the people on the hill. He held one hand high in the air and intoned, "Mary Jane McMinn has just accepted Jesus as her Savior, and I hereby baptize her in the name of the Father, the Son, and the Holy Spirit."

Amos dunked her under the water and brought her back up; then he turned her to introduce her to the crowd on the hill. "May I present to you our new sister in Christ!"

The crowd began to shout as they jumped up and ran forward. They rushed into the water with the two, singing and hugging one another. Mary Jane looked in wonder from face to face. Amazed, she realized that she really did feel different.

Sixteen

After Ross crossed the Red River going into Texas, the country turned to gentle rolling hills dotted with the big cottonwoods that grew so well in the river basins. They were bare to the sky, a testament to the onslaught of winter. The skies above showed winter as well, gray and foreboding, with an occasional hint of a snowflake in the air.

Ross dug out the lined denim jacket from his blanket roll and slipped into it, turning up the collar to cut the wind. Off to his left he saw the glow of a campfire, and he took an angle toward it. As he got close, he hailed it.

"Hello the camp!"

A menacing voice came from the dark,

accompanied by the sound of the lever working on a Winchester. "Come in slow, stranger, and keep both hands where we can see them."

"No problem, I'm right peaceable." Ross rode in slow, hands holding the reins high.

"Ross, is that you?"

"Who is that?" He held one hand up to shade the glow of the fire so he could make out the man back-lit by the blaze. He couldn't, but he could make out the face of the man on the other side of the fire. "Scott? What are you guys doing over this way?"

"We're still in the 'easy work but good money' business," Scott said. "Got our eye on a bank over at Fort Worth."

Ross rode into the clearing and stepped down. "Howdy, Jack, Slim. I take it Wilbur is setting up the job?" He walked his horse to the picket line strung on the edge of the clearing.

"Yeah, he's in town." Scott jerked his thumb in the general direction of Fort Worth.

"He ain't gonna be setting fire to the place, is he? I don't think I liked that much."

"Neither did those XIT ranch hands," said Jack. "That's how we came over this way. Them yahoos were riding in packs all over that whole neck of the woods, with a rope hanging from every saddle. We didn't like the odds."

Ross tied his horse off on the picket line, dropped the saddle, rubbed him down with the saddle blanket, then moved to the fire, rubbing his hands. "It's starting to get a little raw out."

He squatted at the fire and poured himself a cup

of coffee before he asked, "What's the plan?"

Scott pulled his blanket up over his shoulders and got up. "In case you ain't been watching that cloud bank north of us, I figure we got a rip-snortin' snowstorm blowing in on us."

"I been figuring that way too. Hoped to make Fort Worth before it hit." He blew on the coffee, tried a tentative sip, then resumed blowing on it again.

Scott walked over to the fire to sit next to Ross. "When it does hit, that town is gonna button up tighter than a pair of long johns on a frosty morning. We're going to blow in right in the teeth of the storm, hit that bank, and sail out of town with the wind to our back. We'll leave those bankers tied up snug, and by the time anybody is the wiser, there won't be a single track to see."

"Sounds like a bad ride, but it also sounds like it might work." Ross warmed his hands at the fire. It seemed to be getting colder by the minute.

"Won't be that bad. There's an old man down south of here that used to ride the owlhoot trail. He's barely making it, and we can ride out the storm at his place. For a few bucks, he'll keep his mouth shut."

"Guess I can eat a little snow for a good payday."

"Not so fast. What about that ranger that was dogging your trail?"

"He ain't dogging nothing right now. I put some lead in him."

"That so?" They looked at Ross with newfound respect. They knew Slocum's reputation, and if Ross had shaded him, they figured him for some kind of hand with a gun. "You finish him?"

"Naw, just took him out of action. Them rangers get mighty testy if you kill one of their own."

"That's so, but if you don't, they never give up on a trail."

Ross laughed. "Normally I'd say that's so, but I left this ranger hung up with a situation he's never come up against before. If he can survive the little lady that's caring for him, he'll be an uncommonly lucky man."

They nodded knowingly, having absolutely no idea what he was talking about, but the way he said it made it sound like unassailable truth.

When they found that they all seemed to be going to Fort Worth, the two wagons in the tent revival trailed along with the Campbell wagon. When it came time to stop for the night, they made camp together.

Slocum had been sleeping with James under the wagon since he had recovered enough to be able to get down from it. He left his blanket wrapped around him and hobbled over to the fire. Mary Jane was busy preparing a meal, and James, Amos, and Joseph were warming themselves in front of the substantial blaze. There was a definite chill in the air.

"I got to get back on the move," Slocum said to James. "Your brother is getting further and further away."

James handed him a cup of coffee. "I don't figure he's all that far ahead. We've made good miles every day, and you've done all right in the wagon, but up on a horse would be a different thing."

"How do you know? I haven't seen you down studying tracks any."

"I can feel him. He's that way." James pointed south with his cup of coffee.

"When we crossed that river it put us in Texas. I don't figure him for Texas. I figure he headed back to No Man's Land."

"No," James said confidently. "He went this way."

"Your mama said you could do that, feel one another, but I reckon I'm gonna have to see that to believe it."

"I believe it," Amos said. "Since I got religion, I've seen a lot of things that don't make sense except by faith. I've seen people who seemed to be able to read each other's minds, finish each other's sentences. This isn't such a stretch."

Slocum looked skeptical. "Well, be that as it may, you realize that when that cloud bank catches up to us, we're going to be hip deep in snow, don't you?"

"That's why I've been pushing so hard," said James. "I'd like to ride this out in town."

"That'd be Fort Worth, or maybe Clarksboro, over that way." Slocum made a sort of gesture to point with one of the hands holding the blanket tight.

James nodded knowingly. "That's where Ross is."

"The storm'll be on us before we get there. You don't understand. There ain't nothing between us and the North Pole but a few strands of barbed wire. When those things hit, they come at'cha sideways, and they can cause what we call a 'whiteout,' where you can't see anything but white anywhere you look.

Impossible to find your way."

"Long as I got Ross out there to lead the way, I'll stay on course."

Slocum shook his head. It was clear he didn't believe.

Mary Jane came up behind him. "My, but that fire feels good. You need to keep this blanket up over your sore shoulder." She adjusted the blanket up around him more. As she did so, her foot kicked the tail of the blanket into the coals at the edge of the fire.

"I'm gonna let Ma sleep as long as she will," she added, opening the lid to the cook box. "I'll get us something to eat. How do skillet cakes sound?" She got a bowl out and began beating up a batter.

A few minutes later, flames started licking up Slocum's back. "Yeow ... ouch ... ouch ... what the ...!" James jumped to his aid and beat the flames out with his own blanket.

They sat there in silence for a few moments. Finally Slocum said, "I'm kinda having a run of bad luck."

"Me too," James agreed. He looked over at Mary Jane, humming as she prepared breakfast. "You know, Ross thinks she's a jinx."

"Her?" Slocum said. "She ain't had nothing to do with any of *my* bad luck."

"Mine neither; she was never anywhere around when things happened. He's just looking for somebody to blame for his own carelessness."

"Yup."

Seventeen

For more than a day, the gang had been waiting on the outskirts of town for the storm to build to sufficient intensity that it would hide their nefarious activity. When it happened, the storm went from not strong enough to all they could possibly handle in a matter of minutes.

The snow began to blow so hard they could scarcely see beyond the heads of their horses. They had to dismount and lead the animals, practically feeling their way. They lost direction several times but finally found their way into town.

"We may have figured this wrong," Scott yelled. "I ain't sure we can find the old man's place in this blizzard."

"We can wait until it starts to break," Jack suggested.

Scott shook his head. "No good. We do that, and instead of hiding our tracks, it'll make such a clear trail a three-year-old could run us to ground. We gotta do it now or call it off."

"What we need is a compass," Ross interjected. "You say the old man's place is due south?"

Scott shook his head. "More like south by southeast."

"If we had a compass, wouldn't it get us close enough to find our way in?"

"I think so, if we got there before the fences drifted over. Could get tough to find after that."

"We better get 'er done then. You guys do the bank, and I'll go get us a compass at the store."

They tied the horses on the leeward side of the building out of the wind and split up. Ross felt his way along the buildings, trying to find something by which he could recognize the store. He finally found it, but the store was closed. *Even better. Nobody to identify me. Wonder if they live over it? No matter, this wind is so loud they ain't likely to hear me.*

He wrapped his muffler around his hand and broke the small window in the back door. He stepped inside and stood still, listening for any sound of alarm. He couldn't hear anything but the wind. *Well, if I can't hear them, they can't hear me.*

He lit a match and began to ease his way around the room. He soon found a glass-topped counter that contained the item he wanted, and a nice pocket watch as well. *Oh well, long as I'm here.*

* * *

"I don't like to say I told you so," Slocum had his bandanna up over his nose, so his voice was muffled. "Definitely a whiteout."

James walked, leading the team, as he picked his way through the snow.

"I don't see how you can tell where you're going," Slocum shouted, peering ahead but failing to see James until he suddenly appeared beside him. The other two wagons were not visible behind them, even though the rope tying them together was still taut. It wasn't there to pull them, but simply to serve as a guide.

"Let's not go through that again. I can feel the direction; I just have to make sure we don't run over something on the way."

"Allowing for a minute that might be true, and I ain't saying I believe it is, what if your brother is lost in this mess? Doesn't that make you lost too if you are following him?"

The surprise on James's face was clear. "I hadn't thought about that possibility. I'll give you that. Any more of that coffee?"

They had built a small fire inside a bucket in the wagon, small enough that it wouldn't be in danger of catching the wagon on fire, but big enough to keep the coffee hot and to warm the inside of the wagon. James climbed up to warm his hands and to drink a little coffee to warm his insides.

Amos stuck his head in the back. "Thought I'd check to see why we stopped. Everything all right?"

"Just taking a quick break, Preacher. Climb on up here."

Mary Jane put her warm hands on James's cheek. "You're freezing. Why are you going on? Shouldn't we stop and wait it out?"

"I don't think so. I'm afraid the mules would freeze to death. If I keep them moving, they stand a better chance of staying warm enough to survive."

"I agree," Amos said. "Keeping moving is our only chance. I believe in you, but you won't take it as a lack of faith if we continue to pray about it, will you?"

"Can't have too much prayer, Preacher," James said. "I appreciate it."

"I gotta spell you off." Slocum shrugged off the blanket. "I've knitted enough to do it."

James put a hand on him to keep him from rising. "Maybe so, but can you sense the direction?"

"No, but I ain't convinced that you can either."

"You're just going to have to trust me on that one."

Amos smiled. "Come on, Brother Slocum. Trust is what my faith is built on."

"I hope you have enough for the both of us."

Amos laughed. "If necessary, I may have. Come on, James, let's get back to it, and we'll trust in the Lord and that strange connection you have with your brother."

"Close that door! Were you born in a barn?" The teller sat huddled by a glowing potbellied stove. He didn't know why he was still there; he figured it was mostly because the skinflint banker was afraid he would miss a dollar's worth of business by closing for the storm.

He got up to go to his cage. He didn't think about the bandannas and mufflers pulled up over his visitors' faces because of the cold. Then he saw the guns in their hands.

"Not again," the teller said dejectedly.

Scott caught the comment. "Again? You been held up before?"

"Twice."

"What's your name, friend?"

"Michael." He was a young man, about twenty-six, bookish, with wire-rimmed spectacles. He didn't look to be the heroic type. Scott didn't figure him for trouble.

"Well, Michael, you work with us here, and you can get back to your nice warm fire without any significant holes in you. With this wind blowing out here, we could shoot you, and nobody would be any the wiser."

"I'll give you no trouble. There's a gun under this counter. Just to show my good faith, I'm going to bring it out with two fingers and set it on the counter."

Scott took the gun and replaced it with a pair of saddlebags. "We're going to get along just fine, Michael. Now fill these bags up."

"All I've got is what is here in the cage. I can't open the safe."

"This safe?" Jack tried the handle, and it opened.

"Well, what do you know? I suppose the time lock hasn't set yet. I thought it had."

"That's all right, Michael. I know you wouldn't mislead us on purpose. Why don't you get back to your stove while we do a little business here. You don't mind if Jack ties you up a bit, do you?"

"I find that highly preferable to getting shot."

"Let's do 'er that way then."

Scott gathered up the money while Jack tied the teller snugly to the chair. Jack said, "Hope somebody comes and finds you before that stove goes out."

"I don't suppose you'd stoke it up a bit before you leave?" Michael said hopefully.

"Don't mind a bit," Jack said. "Lemme toss in some fresh coal." The little tin scoop made a scrunching sound as he put several scoops on the fire and closed the door.

"That'd make the banker as mad as robbing him is gonna do."

"What'cha mean, Michael?"

"Three whole scoops on the fire, all at one time? He'll faint dead away. Did I mention he was as cheap as they come?"

"I believe it. Are those knots all right? Are you comfortable?"

"I'm fine, given the circumstances. I have to say, you are the most agreeable bank robbers that I've ever encountered."

"We aim to please."

"Hey!" James shouted into the wind.

Slocum parted the canvas to look out. "What's the matter?"

"We're blocked by some kind of fence, four planks and maybe seven or eight feet tall." James started leading the team to the side looking for a gate.

"I'll be hornswoggled if you haven't found the stock pens. That means we're on the outskirts of Fort Worth. I'd never have believed it if I hadn't seen it myself."

James followed the fence to a large barn. He got the door open and struggled to lead the mules and wagons inside. As the doors closed on man and beast, the relief from the wind was overwhelming. It could still be heard howling outside, but the comparative silence was deafening.

They emerged from the wagons, holding lanterns high. The light poked into the corners of the big barn, revealing a few horses in stalls and a loft full of hay.

"Man, does that feel good or what?" James loosened the muffler around his face.

"I reckon I won't be making fun of your ability to sense your brother anymore. Either that or you're the luckiest man I ever met."

Eighteen

James pitched some hay for the mules.

Amos and Slocum came over to help. Slocum removed the sling and worked his arm gingerly to loosen up the muscles.

"I'll settle up with the owner in the morning," James said, even though it didn't need to be voiced.

"Let's get these ladies over to the hotel," the lawman said. "I know the way from here."

James eyed the resolute look on Slocum's face. "You look like you're expecting trouble."

"I don't know what to expect, but I figure on being ready."

They looked over toward the other wagons. "Are you coming with us?" James asked Amos.

Amos shook his head. "I don't think so. I did a few things here back in the old days. I have to be very careful how I approach the sites of my earlier escapades. I'll try to get with the sheriff before we meet too many people."

"It's mighty cold in here."

"There's a forge over there that I can build the heat up in, and we have a small stove in our camp wagon. I think we'll be fine."

"All right, but if the cold starts getting to be too much, you come on over to the hotel," Slocum said. "I'll take care of the sheriff."

James and Slocum locked arms with Ma and Mary Jane, and the four of them followed the line of the buildings until they reached the hotel. The blowing snow was knocked down a bit by the buildings in town, the visibility slightly better.

They banged on the bell sitting on the counter until they roused the clerk. He looked as if he wasn't fully awake as he pushed the register toward them to sign in. With only a brief glance at the names, he turned to pull a key for one room for the ladies and another for the room the two men would share.

The men walked the ladies to their room; then instead of going into the other room, Slocum pulled his pistol and checked the loads. "You going somewhere?" James asked.

"I need to know why the lights are lit in the bank this time of night, particularly with this storm." He replaced the pistol in his holster.

"I'll go with you," James said as he picked up his shotgun.

"I didn't ask you to."

"I'm not asking permission."

Every so often they would stop, light the lantern beneath the cover of a blanket, and check the compass. It was a nuisance, but Ross couldn't figure any other way to do it. The wind was so strong that, without the blanket, it blew the lantern out in short order.

When they moved, they strung out single file, each man holding the tail of the horse in front of him. The north wind howled at their back. Even with the horses in the lead breaking a trail through the snow, it was nearly waist deep, and wading through it was exhausting.

When they stopped to huddle around the compass again, Slim said, "Somebody tell me again what a good plan this is. I'm freezing to death, and we could come within ten foot of a house and never know it."

"You guys are going to have to move your hands away from this lantern long enough for me to read the compass," Ross growled. "It ain't like it's giving off all that much heat anyway."

"I don't want anybody to think I'm one of them kind of fellers," Jack said, "but all of us huddling up under this blanket feels pretty good."

Scott gave him a hard look. "You just keep both hands where I can see them."

"According to this compass, we're on course," Ross assured him. "But good idea or not, we're committed now. We've got to get to that cabin or freeze to death right here where we stand."

"Nobody's arguing that point," Scott said. "We gotta keep moving or die."

Slocum and James burst in the back door of the bank.

"Again?" Michael said. "You're too late—I've already been cleaned out. You guys are going to have to start making appointments."

Slocum pinned on his badge and pulled his bandanna down from his face. "That mean you've been robbed?"

"Couple of hours ago, maybe more. I've kinda lost track of time." James crossed the room to untie him. The clerk stood to stomp his feet in order to restore circulation.

"How many were there?"

When the numbness started subsiding in his feet, the young teller turned his attention to briskly rubbing his hands for the same purpose. "I saw three was all."

"This one of them?" Slocum produced a handbill on Ross. He held it in front of the teller's nose. The sketch on the bill was so vague that it always surprised the ranger when anybody recognized a person from it.

Michael put on his spectacles and studied it. "Hard to be sure. They were masked, but I'd have to say no, even at that."

Slocum folded it back up. "Strange, I'd have bet money on it."

The band of outlaws found a fencerow and followed it. They came to a house, and Scott went to the door to check. He came back to say, "Not it, but the man said if we'd pick up that fencerow right over there and stay with it, it'd take us where we want to go. He said we could put up here until the storm broke."

"That was mighty nice of him," Ross said. "We might oughta do what he says."

Scott shook his head. "I don't think it'd be a good idea for us to get caught here. We'd best stick to the plan."

Slim cast a nervous look at the closed door. "I don't like it. He'll put the law onto us, sure as shootin'."

"Trust me, he ain't putting nobody on to nuthin'. That's why we'd better not get caught here."

Ross frowned. "I didn't sign on for no killin'."

"So stay here."

They moved out, and this time Ross brought up the rear. He was no saint, but he had standards, and killing people if any other alternative was possible was crossing the line for him. He resolved to break company with this bunch as soon as the opportunity presented itself.

Amos and Judy found the sheriff and made arrangements to have a revival meeting in the barn when the weather broke. The sheriff was openly skeptical that Amos had reformed, but Judy was an unimpeachable character witness.

Over at the hotel, James studied the ranger's face. "You figuring to go after them?" They had just gotten back to their room and were removing their stiff, frozen coats.

Slocum pulled off his gloves and alternated blowing in his hands and rubbing them together. James did the same.

"No. By my calculations, we stretched our luck as far as we reasonably can in getting here," Slocum said. "I'll wait 'til the storm breaks, then I'll get after them."

James rubbed the back of his neck. All this was giving him a headache. "You know there won't be any tracks, right?"

"I know. That's what they're counting on." Slocum started stripping down to his long johns. "It may not be tracks I'm looking for but frozen carcasses."

"No, Ross isn't dead. If he were, I'd know it," said James. He sat down on the bed while Slocum stepped across his leg, facing away from him. James put his foot on the ranger's rump and pushed to help him remove the wet boots.

"More of that mumbo jumbo?" Slocum stood holding the wet boots as he looked James in the face. He was dead serious as he spoke. "Still, it sure enough brought us through that storm. Can't say I believe even yet, but I'm open to the idea that there might be something to it."

James smiled. "You're coming around." They traded places so James could help pull off Slocum's boots.

"I'll tell you what I want to come around to, and it's that nice warm bed over there. You don't steal covers, do you?"

Nineteen

*I*t took two days for the storm to blow itself out. Snow was piled up to the eaves on most structures. In open areas, it was still chest high for a tall horse. Cooped up in the old man's house, the outlaws were beginning to snap at each other.

"I don't want to hear any more about killing that rancher. I'm tired of it. What's done is done." Scott glared at Ross, daring him to respond.

Ross knew when to let well enough alone. "Well, I know that ranger is after me again by now, and I figure you don't want any part of that. It's probably best that I ride out alone as soon as it's possible."

Scott nodded. "You got that right. If Bulldog Slocum is around, I want him after you, not me." The outlaw studied Ross. He had considered removing the source of his irritation and increasing the split of the money for the rest of them at the same time.

Slocum was the joker in the deck though. It would be worth it to let Ross ride away to serve as bait for the lawman. He made up his mind. He wouldn't kill him after all. If he would shut up, that is.

Slim stood at the window. "Sun's coming out. It'll be starting to thaw now."

The desire to be on the trail was driving Slocum crazy. It had been pleasant hanging around the hotel, eating in the dining room, enjoying the company of Mary Jane. There had been the matter of that waiter breaking a whole tray of dishes, but he still didn't give credence to the theory that she might be a jinx. Something like that could happen to anybody, and the waiter wasn't anywhere near her when it happened.

Slocum had found himself entertaining thoughts lately of home and hearth. Mary Jane was the kind of girl to make a man think about giving up his badge or at least consider settling down to marshal a town so he could be home every night. He wondered if he had a chance with her.

Perhaps this was his opportunity to find out. He was alone with her in the dining room, as James had gone to walk his mother to her room. *A man doesn't get anything he doesn't ask for,* he thought.

"What are your plans now?" he inquired.

Mary Jane regarded him frankly. "I honestly don't know. I still feel like I should pursue Ross until

I know for sure what his story is, but the more I find out about him ... oh, I don't know. How could I love a man who is outside the law?"

"That's what I've been wondering. I'm pleased you're at least thinking about it." His collar felt tight. His voice sounded husky to him. He swallowed hard and decided to go for it. "Could you ever love a man *inside* the law? A man that wore a badge?"

"Why, Mr. Slocum, do you have anybody in mind?" She suddenly became very coquettish and hid a smile behind her napkin.

"Of course I do, and you know it." Slocum wasn't equipped for this verbal sparring. He was a man who said what he thought, flat out, and the Devil take the hindmost. He was not accustomed to having someone toy with him. "I'm thinking I have feelings for you, and I'm looking to find out if you feel anything for me."

"Are you looking for me to declare myself? With no prior hint that any such thing was brewing? That's rather presumptuous of you, Mr. Slocum."

He felt as if he had been penned, and someone was heating a branding iron. *How did I get myself into this situation?* "No, of course not. I just wanted you to know how I felt so you could start thinking about it."

"I shall think about it, Mr. Slocum. You have given me a great deal to think about indeed."

James returned to the dining room. He looked at the two of them as he took his seat. Something was going on—there was electricity in the air. Slocum was as flushed as if he had been caught making a run to the outhouse in his long johns. Mary Jane looked amused but excited at the same time.

"Did I miss something?" James asked.

Slocum got to his feet. "Harummmph, not that I know of. I was just about to go talk to the town marshal about going after those bank robbers." With that, he turned on his heels and fled the scene.

James sat down, perplexed. He put the feeling from his mind. He relaxed, let out a deep breath, and changed the subject. "Well, it appears Ross has gotten away from us again. What do you think we ought to do now?"

Mary Jane was still feeling playful. "People certainly are interested in my opinions tonight."

He frowned. "What does that mean?"

"Mr. Slocum just asked me the same kind of question, what I thought *we* should do, only the we he was interested in involved a different pairing."

"He did, did he?" He looked in the direction the ranger had gone, though he could no longer see him. "I guess he had some thoughts on what you should do?"

She smiled and began to pay close attention to her dessert fork, inspecting it as if it had some minute imperfection. "He might have had a suggestion or two."

I'll just bet he did. "And did these suggestions have anything to do with him playing a part in your life?"

Her eyes came up slowly. She cocked her head slightly. "Why, James, you are inquiring about what is surely a very personal communication."

"Very personal, is it?" *I was right. Slocum is trying to move in on her. What is with this girl? First my* no-good brother, now some footloose lawman with no place to lay his head? Why can't she see what's right under her nose?

"James, you are acting very much as if you are jealous. Are you?" *My, my,* she thought, *why am I wasting my time pursuing somebody who doesn't seem to want me when there seems to be such a selection of eligible suitors at hand?* She measured James with her eyes. *I wonder why I never considered James this way? He looks just like Ross; only he's considerate, gentle, and attentive. Perhaps it's just because he has always been there, always been my confidant, my friend. Right now, he looks as if he has just swallowed a frog.*

James was indeed uncomfortable. Pushed into a corner with no warning, he had been asked to own up to feelings he hadn't even been willing to admit to himself. His natural self-defense sprang into play. "Jealous? Me? Don't be silly."

He is *jealous. My goodness. This puts a whole new light on things.* "Well, if you aren't inquiring out of a personal motive, then I suppose you are asking to see if I intend to continue traveling with you."

That remark gave him an out, and he took it gratefully. "Yes, that's it. Are you leaving our company?"

"Not at present. I am having second thoughts about Ross, I'll admit, but I have not yet given up the idea. Has your mother given up on the idea of catching him?"

His shoulders fell slightly. He sounded disconsolate as he answered. "No, she's as determined as ever."

"Then we will leave things as they are for the time being. Is that satisfactory?"

It is indeed. He got to his feet. "It's fine with me, but we'd best go check on Ma."

She got out of her seat while he put money on the table. They walked across the dining room, but when they got to the door, Mary Jane pulled up short and simply waited, her purse held in both hands in front of her.

It took James a moment or two to understand that she was waiting for him to open the door for her. When it dawned on him, he stepped around her, swung the door open with a pronounced bow, and swept his hat in a gesture to show her the way.

"Allow me, miss."

"Why, thank you, kind sir."

When James made his fine gesture, he came rump to rump with the waiter serving the table just to the left of the door. The waiter was showing a very attractive cheesecake to the occupants of the table, trying to interest them in having dessert.

As the waiter was leaning forward to exhibit the cheesecake, it did not take much of a shove to put him off balance, and the nudge from James was quite sufficient. He fell forward spread-eagle on the table. The faces of the diners turned upward to watch the flight of the gorgeous cheesecake. A matronly lady stared wide eyed as she realized she was in the direct path of the flying confection, but she had no time to take evasive action.

It hit her dead center in the face, then slowly slid down to her generous bodice. She sat there transfixed, as did everyone at the table. Unthinkable. Then her husband did something even more unthinkable ... he laughed. More to the point, he completely lost his composure, almost sliding from his chair to slip underneath the table.

The waiter recovered and started futile efforts to clean up the offending mess, making clucking, embarrassed noises as he did so. He only succeeded in making it worse, and his efforts to accomplish the task, without touching anything he should not touch, were terribly obvious and added to the glee of the onlookers.

There are those who can laugh at themselves and join in the fun. This lady was not one of them. She scraped the bulk of the mess from her face, looked at the gaping mouth of her husband, and let him have it. He was powerless to resist. The entire dining room exploded in laughter.

Poised to exit the dining room, James and Mary Jane looked back in wonder. "This place has been a disaster all evening," Mary Jane observed. "They really should do something about training their staff."

Twenty

A surprising number of people braved the snowdrifts to come to the tent meeting. Those who did come knew of Amos, and he had exploited many of them. They were not convinced that this meeting was not simply another one of his schemes.

The accumulated snow prohibited putting up the tent, but they were able to modify the livery barn for their purposes. Once emptied of the lumber to make the benches, the freight wagon was pulled across the end of the barn to make something of a stage, just as with the tent arrangement. The left-hand sideboard of the wagon dropped down, and supports went under it to create a small stage. The pump organ was permanently mounted behind the driver's seat, and

Judy played it from there.

They slipped a couple of tall boards into the brackets, stringing up the wagon cover to provide a backdrop.

Amos lit the lanterns. The soft glow reflected around the barn. He looked over to where they had pulled the lumber from the wagon and put the benches together. It made a very presentable little church.

He stopped behind the stage to compose himself and pray. Judy stepped up and got the organ going. Joseph led those who had gathered in several well-known songs, his rich baritone voice rising above the sound of the whole crowd, not to mention the organ.

Joseph gave the opening prayer. "Dear Lord," he said, one arm upraised, "we come to You this evening, asking for Your presence here among us. Father in heaven, Amos is here in obedience to Your will. These people know what a sinner he is. He knows that without You he is nothing. If he is to accomplish anything at all here tonight, it will only be if You fill him with Your Spirit and give him the words You would have him say. We turn the service over to You now and pray that You will move among us in a mighty way."

Joseph generally used similar words to set the stage for Amos to try and make amends to those who were sure to be in attendance. Every time they returned to a town where Amos had pursued his wicked ways, there were always suspicions to be overcome.

Amos stopped at the small podium and smiled.

He had settled on what he thought to be the best way to overcome this obstacle as well. "I'm not here because I'm a good man. You know better. I couldn't fool you if I tried. I'm here as a really bad man that God decided to use anyway. I'm here not because of anything I have done, but because of what He has chosen to do through me."

Amos opened the worn, old Bible. "Those of you who have your Bibles might want to turn to John 5:19." There was a gentle whisper as some, mostly the ladies, turned the pages.

"'Verily, verily, I say unto you, The Son can do nothing of himself, but what he seeth the Father do: for what things soever he doeth, these also doeth the Son likewise.'"

Amos looked up and held the old book out to them. "You get what this is saying? Jesus Himself is saying that *He is nothing without God*. If *He* says that, how much less than nothing can I be? I mean that makes me feel like I could walk right under a snake with my tallest hat on."

He paused to let them get a good mental picture of that image. "You know, back when I was disguised and fooling people doing this, I could never fool Joseph. I tried to. I did my best to make him think I had come to believe, but he never went for it. He said I couldn't fool him if it wasn't true and that I couldn't hide it if it was. I hope that's true, because it's all that's standing between me and your scorn. If you can see Jesus in me, then you know it's Him reaching out to you, not me."

He stepped down from the stage and gave an

altar call, but nobody came forward. When he finished, the congregation filed out quietly.

"Not much of a reaction," Amos said.

"Same thing every time; they're still making up
their mind, give them time," Joseph said.

"Fortunately it isn't up to me. If the Lord is working on them, they'll come around."

"Exactly."

Twenty-one

Sheriff Jackson was not strongly motivated to brave the freezing weather to go after the bandits. The sheriff's office was warm and comfortable. When Slocum burst in, the sheriff sat napping, feet up on his desk. A small man, Jackson's stomach bulged out between his suspenders, gray walrus mustache fluttering as he snored.

Slocum slammed the door against the cold wind. Jackson jerked awake, and the action sent him over backward; the contact jammed his hat down over his face. Slocum walked over to peer behind the desk. "You all right?"

Jackson jerked the hat off with some effort and sputtered, "Of course, of course, you just startled me, is all. I didn't expect anybody to be out in such weather." He got up, methodically dusting himself off.

"Well, it ain't like I wanna be out, but the longer we hole up, the further them bank robbers is getting away." He walked over to the glowing little stove and poured himself a cup of noxious-looking coffee. He sniffed the offensive brew, took a tentative sip, and set the cup aside.

Jackson smirked at the gesture. "Yeah, that coffee is nasty. I've been sitting here steeling myself to deal with that hell-on-wheels banker. He's gonna bust through that door any minute now wanting to know why I haven't recovered his money." He repositioned his chair carefully, sat down in it, then rocked it back onto two legs.

The ranger grabbed the chair across the desk from the sheriff, spun it around backward, then mounted it like a horse. He leaned his forearms across the back of the chair. "What is it you're going to tell him?"

The sheriff shrugged. "What can I tell him? That because of this dad-blamed storm them boys is long gone."

Slocum frowned. "I don't agree. I'm sure they toughed it out for a while to try to put some distance between us, but that would have been a gut-busting ride. They couldn't have kept it up for long, before they would've had to go to ground too."

"You may be right." Jackson groomed his mustache with his forefinger. He wasn't used to having his opinions questioned.

"Ain't no maybe to it, Sheriff. Earliest they could have hit the trail was when the weather broke last night."

Jackson's excuses were getting more and more feeble. "You know there won't be any tracks; that's why they did it when they did, so the blowing snow would cover their trail."

"That was smart, all right, but they didn't think it through. The tracks will be covered to where they holed up, but a blind man could track them when they get back on the trail. You'd best start getting you a posse together so we can get after them."

"I reckon so." He looked toward the frosted window on the front of the little building. "I sure hate the thought of getting out in this weather."

The door slammed back on its hinges, and a well-dressed, red-faced businessman stormed into the room. Snow from the porch swirled around the room, and the cozy warmth was gone immediately. "Jackson! Why haven't you recovered my money yet?"

Slocum smiled and walked to the door. "I'll just leave you two alone. You'll find me at the livery stable when you're ready to go."

Ross rode out from the hideout right after the storm broke, as he had promised. He rode back toward town until he hit the main road. He smiled as he noted that there had already been some traffic on it. His tracks wouldn't be as noticeable. "It won't fool that ranger long, but every little bit helps."

He swung back south, looking over his shoulder

and nodding with satisfaction at the way his horse's hoofprints blended in with the other tracks. The snow was still more than knee high on his big sorrel, so the going would be slow, but it would be just as slow for any pursuers.

He had half-expected trouble getting his cut of the loot, but Scott had handed it right over. *I guess he was so eager to get me out of there to avoid a run-in with Slocum, that he wasn't in a mood to argue.*

The trees were covered with ice, but the bright sun was already beginning to melt it. The wet ice reflected the sun's rays and made the trees appear to be encrusted with diamonds. *It won't take long to melt the snowpack if this weather keeps up,* thought Ross. His breath hung in the air in front of him, but it wasn't an uncomfortable ride.

If the wind would slack off, it'd be pretty pleasant out here. He looked at the wet surface of the snowbanks. *That's already starting to melt. If I can stay ahead of Slocum until this turns to mud and slush, I think I can shake him off me.*

James rarely argued with his mother, but he had to take a hard stand this time. "Ma, we just can't do it. I know the posse is pulling out, and I can ride with them if you want, but we can't keep up with them in the wagon."

He walked to the window of the hotel room and gestured at the snowdrifts outside. "If we had a sleigh, them mules could pull it in this deep snow, but the wagon would break them down in a matter of miles. They couldn't do it."

Her anguish was clear on her face as she joined him at the window. "It just weighs on me that Ross was so close, and now he's getting away before I can spend some time with him."

James put his arm around her thin shoulders. "I know it does, Ma, and I know why you want to spend time with him. I know you figure his evil ways are dragging him straight to the pit. I figure you aim to remind him back to his upbringing."

"Yes," she gave him a weak smile. "I can't rest if I don't at least give it a try. You know, a person can wait too long and get a hardened heart. It's all over then."

"Don't fret yourself, Ma. You know Ross can't get away from me. I can always tell where he's going."

Twenty-two

*R*aise your right hand." Sheriff Jackson swore in eleven men, not counting Slocum and himself. They were hard men, the softer ones being safe at home by their fireplaces. "Anybody need ammunition? The county is buying. Wouldn't do to run out when we catch up to them outlaws." His words hung in the air in little white puffs.

A rancher showed concern in his eyes. "You expecting a fight, Edgar? I ain't shot at nobody in a coon's age."

"Sure hope not, Hank, but it's best to be prepared. Expect the worst, and you'll generally be pleasantly surprised, I always say."

The group swung out of the stable yard in a

ragged line, Jackson and Slocum in the lead. James had left the choice up to his mother as to whether he should ride with them. She decided against it.

The group rode for a couple of miles before Slocum pulled up. "Let's be smart about this, boys. If we keep this up, the sheriff and I are going to be walking soon. You know how ducks take turns leading the flock so the ones in the front won't get so tired? Seems to me it'd be a right good idea if we took turns breaking the trail through this snow."

Hank pulled up beside him. "How about we switch off every twenty minutes or so?" Slocum added.

"I got no idea where we're going," Hank said.

"Nobody else does either. I'm thinking they couldn't have stood that blinding snow more'n two or three hours the other night, and they couldn't have been making good time. My hunch is they went to ground within ten miles, so if we go out that far, then try to cut a trail, we oughta be in business."

Hank nodded and rode out. About ten minutes later he pulled up. "Hey, Ranger. I ain't the sharpest tool in the shed, but if all we're doing is getting out a ways where we can cut across and try to pick up their trail, wouldn't it be even easier if we crossed over and followed the road 'til we get out there where we want to be?"

Slocum dropped his head. Finally he looked up, a sheepish grin spreading across his face. "I thought I was pretty smart to think of swapping off the lead. Reckon I feel dumb as a cow patty about now."

They all laughed and swung over to intersect the

road. When they got to it, Slocum pulled up and said, "Never figured this many people to be out yet." He sat there studying the road, deep in thought.

"What's on your mind, Ranger?" Jackson said.

"Something's nagging at me." He pointed at the tracks. "See how those tracks are crisp in the front but blurred in the back? The horse kinda tosses up a little snow in back when they pick their hoof up. That means the horses were headed toward town."

"So?"

"So, you suppose these jaspers are smart enough to know we'd try to pick them up in the snow and decided to ride back through town the other way?"

Jackson frowned. "Now that there is a scary thought. Didn't see anybody I don't know riding through before we left, so they'd have had to slip by us while we were in the backcountry. That's a pretty slim time frame."

"My fault. We should have come by the road to begin with."

"Don't get all down on yourself about it—one guess was as good as the other." Jackson looked around at the men present and made his selection. "Kendall? How about you ride back to town and see if anybody rode through. If they did, grab a fresh horse and burn the hide off him coming after us. If not, just stay there."

The deputy headed back at as briskly as the depth of the snow would allow. He was pleased. With any luck it would be a wild-goose chase, and he would be sitting by the stove in the saloon in less than an hour.

The posse turned down the road the other way. They rode nearly an hour before Slocum stopped again.

"What'cha got now, Ranger?" Jackson asked.

Slocum indicated a house in the distance with a nod of his head. "Horse tracks coming from that ranch over there, headed for town."

Jackson tucked his gloves into his pocket, pulled out a sack of tobacco and a packet of papers, and started to roll a cigarette. "That's old man Cather's place."

"He have hands working for him?"

"No, he uses a little day help now and then." Jackson licked the seam on the paper to seal it and then set a match to the end of it. He blew out a long stream of smoke, immediately pulling his gloves back on. "He's barely keeping his head above water, near as I can tell."

"If he lives there by himself, and if these are his tracks heading into town, how come there's smoke coming from his fireplace? Do you boys go off and leave a big fire unattended if you're gonna be gone that long?"

Jackson rubbed his chin. "That is peculiar, now that you mention it. How about we have a look?"

"Hold your water, Sheriff. If this means what I think it means, it'd be best if we didn't ride up there all bunched up together." Slocum pulled his Colt and checked to ensure it was loaded. It was an automatic reflex, part of the ritual of going into action, because he had never in his life failed to reload his weapon after cleaning it. The act had a more practical application as working cowboys carried an empty chamber under the hammer as a safety precaution. If they knew action was coming up, they'd make sure they were fully loaded.

In spite of the cold, Slocum left his gloves off to better handle the revolver. "How about you boys split up into two groups and circle this house. I'll give you time to get in position, then I'll ride right up to the front."

"Sounds like a plan," the sheriff said. The men pulled their rifles, levered shells into the chambers, then split up and rode off in two groups.

Jack was keeping watch out of the frosty window. "Scott, there's some riders over on the road."

"What?" The outlaw moved over to pull aside the burlap curtain and wipe the frost from the window so he could see. "Looks like they're splitting up, trying to cut off our trail somewhere."

He moved away from the window. "Nothing to worry about; I told you they'd do that. Long as we stay put, there won't be any tracks to find except for that idiot Ross. They can go chase him. When they all get past us, we'll ride right back through town, pretty as you please."

Jack shook his head. "There's one of them that ain't movin'."

"What?" Scott looked out again. "I see him; he's just sitting there watching the house. Wonder what he's up to?" He headed back to the rickety old table. I'll tell you this, if he decides to ride over to check this house, he's gonna regret it."

Jack still didn't leave his post. "What if that guy is the ranger?"

"Nah, that ranger is after Ross. Them old boys have one-track minds."

"These guys ain't ridin' no circle," said Wilbur, who was looking out a side window.

"Now what?" Scott took a couple of quick steps to look over Wilbur's shoulder. They could see one group turning to head back toward the house. He ran over to the other side window. The other group was closing in from the opposite direction. "This don't look good, boys," Scott said. "Wonder what could have tipped 'em off?"

Jack pulled his pistol and spun the cylinder to check the loads. "Got me, but it looks like the fat's in the fire. What are we gonna do?"

Wilbur levered his rifle. "Stand 'em off. They're out in the open, and we've got cover."

Scott snorted. "Like a rifle bullet won't punch right through the slab boards on this shack. I'm thinking we'd better head to the barn and get saddled before they get set. We'll shoot our way out."

"Now you're making sense," Jack said.

They made a run for the barn while the posse was too far out to shoot and quickly saddled their mounts.

"Where are they now?" Scott asked.

Jack gestured to indicate directions. "Covering all three sides. They've dismounted and taken up firing positions."

Scott frowned. "But not in front?"

"That lone guy is out in front."

"Slocum."

"Has to be." Jack looked like he had lost his last friend. "How come he didn't follow Ross?"

Scott pulled his pistol. "It don't matter. We got him to deal with now."

Wilbur sounded dejected. "I think I'd rather take on the posse."

"Use your head," Scott snapped. "He's just one man."

"One ranger—it ain't the same thing."

Scott pulled his hat tight on his head. "You with me or not?"

"Aw, man-n-n-n-n—" Wilbur whined.

Scott kicked the barn door open with his foot, cocked his pistol, and spurred his horse forward with a rebel yell. The other two followed him, one on each side. They leaned low over the necks of their horses and began to fire.

Slocum pulled a spare pistol from his saddlebag, stepped down from the saddle, and gave his horse a swat to get it out of the line of fire. He cocked both pistols beside his leg as the riders bore down on him. The flame from the pistols was clear as they fired at him. A couple of shots whizzed by, sounding like angry hornets.

He extended his arm fully, taking aim as if on a pistol range. He fired, and Wilbur pitched back off his horse. Jack sat up slightly to see what had happened to his friend, which was a big mistake. Slocum snapped a shot with his left-hand pistol, and Jack slumped forward on the neck of his horse, then slid to the ground.

Scott still came on full bore. He was riding at an angle now, so the body of his horse was between him and the ranger. He fired under the horse's neck like a Comanche brave. Slocum had no shot and didn't want to shoot the horse. *Wait a minute, I do have a shot.*

He sighted, then squeezed the pistol of the big Colt carefully, deliberately. The only thing he could see was the pistol firing at him, and he hit it dead center. It went spinning away, and Scott came partially back up on top of the animal. Pawing with a hand that had no sensation in it, he reached for the rifle in the saddle scabbard. He managed to pull it free, but he couldn't hold on to it with his numb hand, and it clattered to the icy ground. He pulled the horse around to ride back for it, but the ranger's voice cut through the cold. "Don't make me finish it."

Scott pulled up and raised his hands. He was unarmed, and the ranger had a clean shot. The posse rode up and divided themselves among the three outlaws, checking them out, tying their hands.

"I never saw the like, Ranger." Jackson was stunned. "That was a mighty cool piece of work, standing firm while they blazed away at you."

"Hard to hit a man off the back of a bouncing horse, particularly at that range."

"But you hit them."

"I wasn't bouncing."

Twenty-three

*T*hese two are going to live," Hank said. He pointed at Wilbur. "This one's hit pretty hard though."

"See if the old man has a buckboard," Jackson said. "We'll take them back in that." He looked around. "Speaking of the old man, wonder where he is?"

"All these old places have a hidey-hole where they used to duck raiding Indians," said Slocum. "He's probably down there."

"Reckon we ought to root him out?"

Slocum looked around the run-down spread. "Somebody would get shot going down there after him. From the looks of this place, I'd say it's already about all the punishment he can handle."

"Ain't that the truth? You coming back with us?"

Slocum reloaded his pistols, replacing the spare in his saddlebags. "No, I figure I know who made those tracks coming out of this place, and I don't think he rode toward town for long."

The sheriff watched the ranger step up onto his horse. "You haven't got anything tying him to this bank robbery."

Slocum nodded toward the three being loaded on the wagon. "Not unless one of those guys talks, but I don't really need that; I got plenty without it." He reined around tightly and rode out.

Ross was deep in thought. *An ordinary man would lay up and rest that wound for some time yet, maybe take advantage of the pampering he's sure to be getting from Ma and Mary Jane. Slocum ain't an ordinary man though. Mary Jane? What am I thinking?*

The logic of it was inescapable. If she had been hanging around Slocum, he had probably already been scalded, pounded, and plucked by all the things that seem to happen around her. Ross suddenly realized that Slocum would surely be up and gone as quickly as he could sit a horse. Slocum might be on his tail already, just to get clear of her.

The farther Ross got from Fort Worth, the traffic on the road lessened and the more his tracks stood out. He gave the saddlebags a pat. It was good to have such a nice road stake, but Ross was starting to wish he'd just ridden straight through and put an extra day between him and Slocum before the snow started coming down.

Using the snow to cover the robbery had seemed like a right good idea at the time, but now, looking back at these tracks pointing the way to him like a giant finger, it didn't seem so smart.

All right, since that didn't turn out to be the smart play, I'd better come up with something smart now. Just riding and waiting for him to catch up to me, that's not the way to go for sure.

So, what would be smart? What's the last thing that lawman would expect—the very last? He rode in deep thought for more than an hour. Then he cocked his head as a curious grin came over his face. *The dumbest thing I can think of would be to ride right at that ranger.* He swung his horse around and began to retrace his steps.

This is such a dumb idea that he couldn't possibly figure on me doing it.

Mary Jane stood looking out the hotel window, holding the curtain aside. "The posse is coming in. They've got prisoners."

Ma rushed over to the window. "Do they have Ross?"

James opened the window so they could see better. They scrutinized the faces as they rode by. "I don't see him," James said.

"I don't know whether to be happy or sad about that," Mary Jane said, turning concerned eyes on him.

James nodded. "I know what you mean. I'd better get down there and see what's going on."

Ma was already slipping into her coat. "I 'spect we'd all better go."

Ma had been comfortable during her stay in the hotel. Nice, snug rooms, snow piled up on the windows, she hadn't had shortness of breath or cold sweats since the snow had started coming. Going out in public would be different.

It was no problem, hardly anybody was out. Water ran freely off the roof as they stepped out on the hotel porch. The bright sun was melting the snow rapidly. James stepped between them and took each by the arm to steady them as they crossed the slippery surface to the sheriff's office.

As they entered, Sheriff Jackson was just turning the key on the outlaws. He turned to a deputy and said, "Kendall, you'd better go get Doc. He can tend these fellers here, be safer that way." He looked up. "Here now, you ladies shouldn't be here."

Ma pushed her way past the deputy. "I need to ask them some questions."

"Them two ain't up to it. I sent for the doc to tend to them." He looked at Scott. "I reckon this jasper is all right, if he'll talk."

She moved over to the bars to peer into the face of the outlaw. "Was Ross with you?"

Scott gave the sheriff a nervous glance. "Ross who?"

Ma's eyes sparked. "Don't make me come in there, young man. You know very well who I'm talking about."

Scott threw back his head and laughed. "Like I'm going to be scared of some dried-up old lady?" He laughed so hard he started to choke. He coughed and sputtered, then finally regained his wind. "You got sand, lady—I'll give you that."

He sat for a couple of minutes, but Ma never broke eye contact. "Oh, all right. It ain't like I owe him anything. He was with us. That fool ranger was supposed to follow him instead of us, but he didn't."

"Where is he?" Ma took a grip on the bars, afraid of what she might hear.

"He rode out at first light. I guess that ranger did get after him, just too late to do us any good. That ranger is all I ever heard from him, and more, he smoked all of us and didn't turn a hair. I feel for Ross when he catches up to him."

"I found Ranger Slocum to be most polite and courteous," Ma said.

"Lady, you seen a side of him he ain't never showed me. He didn't look all that polite staring down his pistol barrel at me."

"I'm sure you deserved it."

"Oh yeah, I deserved all of that and more, but it don't mean I enjoyed it any. Sheriff, you wanna get this old biddy out of here? She's starting to annoy me."

Jackson scowled at the outlaw. "You'd best mind your manners, or I'll give her that rolling pin out of the kitchen, open the door, and let her in. I figure it wouldn't take her but a couple of minutes to teach you how to treat ladies."

Scott's tough front faded a bit. "Aw, Sheriff, you might not think so, but I had a mama too. I'm just growling a bit. I don't take to my new surroundings too well; tends to make me a little testy." He removed his hat. "I'm sorry, ma'am, I shouldn't go taking it out on you."

"That's quite all right, sonny. You told me what I wanted to know, no matter how reluctantly."

James shepherded them back out of the office. No sooner did Ma hit the boardwalk than she said, "James, we'd better hitch up the wagon and get going."

"The roads are starting to turn to mud now, Ma. Them mules understand mud, but it'd be mighty slow going and real hard on them, not much better than the deep snow would have been. If we give it another day or two, it'll firm up, and we'll make better time."

"I reckon that'd be the wisest thing to do, but I don't like having to sit here and wait."

"I know you don't, Ma, but tomorrow is Sunday anyway, so we wouldn't be traveling. This way we get to take in a real church service. Monday will be soon enough to get on his trail. Besides, he ain't getting no further away."

"What do you mean by that?"

"I can't say, only I've been feeling him getting further and further away. While ago that feeling left me. I don't know what in the world he's up to, but he ain't putting on distance no more."

Twenty-four

*S*locum followed the road at as brisk a pace as the mud allowed. He was determined to narrow the gap. He had watched carefully for any sign of a rider leaving the trail. Tracks couldn't be followed on the muddy trail, but they could still be seen if they left the road.

He had followed one set of tracks leaving the road, but it quickly developed that it was a cowboy returning to his ranch after a night in town. Back on the road, Slocum continued to press on.

It took no great concentration to ride and watch for emerging tracks, and his mind wandered back to town, to Mary Jane. He was thinking how funny it was that he had backed out of that dining room like a fox out of a badger hole when she turned those big eyes on him. One minute he was all set to declare himself, to tell her he wanted to come courting, and the next ...

What happened? One minute I was feeling all mushy and wanting to say something nice to her, and the next minute I was headed out the door with my tail between my legs.

All he knew was it was easier to stand and face that whole gang of outlaws while they rode down on him shooting. He could handle that—but women, that was something entirely different.

Sunday meant church if James, Ma, and Mary Jane were anywhere they could make that happen. Mary Jane loved the services now that she'd gotten right with the Lord. This Sunday was special for Amos, too. To keep from having conflicting services, the local parson had invited him to preach. The chance to be back in an established church felt very good.

They were not used to having a black man in services but practiced tolerance, grudgingly in some corners of the room. Still, few could resist a smile at Joseph's beautiful baritone voice that rang crystal clear above the entire congregation, paired with Judy's equally sparkling soprano.

Feeling good about the progress he had made in healing his standing with the community, Amos pulled his text from the book of Psalms. "David was a man after God's own heart, but he strayed. He let his love for a woman cause him to do some mighty sinful things; in fact, he ended up killing her husband. Some of the greatest things and some of the worst things in the Bible were done in the name of love."

He came out from behind the podium, old worn Bible open in his hand. "Here in the book of Psalms, we find David trying to get right with God again. We tend to forget when we read over here, that these are songs. David wrote a passel of them, and they were sung by all the musicians in his kingdom."

He smiled at Judy. "David did get right with God again, and God forgave him, much as you have forgiven me. I know God forgave me, and it surely wasn't because I deserved it. There are some of you here now that need that forgiveness, and it's there for you."

Amos went on to read from Psalms and show them the forgiveness that was right there before them. Judy smiled back at him. She did love it so when the Spirit moved him so strongly. It felt as if her heart were in her throat and threatened to escape through her mouth if she were but to open it.

Ross rode back the way he had come. He needed a way to get off the road without leaving a trace of it. It was an impossible task, no way to do it.

The farther he rode, the more nervous he got. He sure didn't want to round a bend and find himself face-to-face with Slocum. *Maybe this idea was every bit as dumb as I said it was.*

The road passed through a grove of trees that came right down to the edge of it. Suddenly, thump—

something hit him! He pawed for his right-hand gun, swiveling in the saddle, searching out the threat.

Nothing.

Something icy slid down his neck. He felt the top of his head and discovered that his hat was covered with snow. He took the hat off to shake it free, looking up to see where it had come from, just in time to get a second blast right in the face. It was falling off the trees.

He replaced the hat, got out his bandanna, and wiped his face. Then it registered. He turned off the road and rode back into the grove, picking his way among the dense trees. When he got out of sight of the road, he dismounted, tied off the horse, and followed the trail of his prints.

He picked up a thick stick he could use for a club. At the edge of the road, he began to whack the trees on either side of the path he had made coming through. At each whack, snow fell from the trees, effectively covering the tracks.

Impossible, eh? How's this for disappearing tracks, Slocum? Let's see you spot these tracks with your magic ranger eyes.

He kept moving back into the grove of trees, whacking tree trunks all the way. The noise made his horse skittish, and he pulled on the reins as he approached, hitting everything in sight.

"Easy, now. I ain't gonna hit you with this." He tossed the stick down and caressed the animal's neck. "Look back behind you there—far as that ranger knows, you've done sprouted wings and flown away."

Later Ross watched as the ranger rode by. He was gesturing with his free hand and talking aloud, although Ross couldn't make out the words. Slocum didn't take a second look at the trail covered with the fresh snowfall from the trees.

Mary Jane, Ross thought. *She's the only one that can make a man that crazy. I almost feel sorry for the guy. Almost.*

Ross gave the ranger fifteen minutes to be sure he was gone, then rode back to the road, and then turned toward Fort Worth. "Horse, it may not make much sense to you, but sometimes the dumbest thing you could possibly do might just turn out to be the smartest thing you could do. Ain't life funny?"

It was dusk by the time Ross reached the outskirts of Fort Worth. He got off the road. He would wait until full dark then slip through town. He could ride around, but if anybody saw him, they would be sure to alert the law. No, it would be safer just to wait until full dark, then he should be able to ease right through.

He wished he could take the time to see his ma, but at the same time he knew it wasn't the smart play. He rode into town at a slow walk, taking side streets. The military post fronted the city so closely that it formed one side of the courthouse square. Wouldn't do to get too close to that; a sentry would be sure to cry out. He stopped and looked. He listened in the darkness and heard nothing but a dog barking in the distance.

That's the back of the hotel. I could slip in that way and see her. No, that do-gooder brother of mine would probably turn me in. His halo is on way too tight.

He sat there for some time staring at the darkened structure. Inside he felt a longing he didn't understand, a need to go make that connection, even though he knew the risk.

Finally, reluctantly, he reined the horse around and walked the animal slowly out of town. He set a course north by northwest toward No Man's Land. *I'll take the high route to Mexico. Slocum will never figure on me doing that.*

Twenty-five

*C*an you believe that feller is coming to tote our bags for us? I told him I'd take care of it, but he said his boss would be mad if he didn't do his job." James's astonishment was written all over his face.

"I can't get used to big-city ways," Ma agreed.

"Is your luggage ready?" A young man with a pill-box hat and a jacket with two rows of bright buttons stood at the door.

James said, "Reckon so."

The young man gathered the tattered bags under his arms and headed for the stairs. He stopped at the door to let Ma go ahead of him. Mary Jane noticed that he hadn't picked up Ma's umbrella. She stuck it in the retaining straps of the suitcase in his left hand.

He felt something and glanced back. She flashed a smile at him, and he returned it with one of his own.

The porter whistled as he headed for the stairs. Ma waited to hold James's arm as she went down, so the porter went ahead, skipping down three steps before the handle of the umbrella caught the railing. He never knew what hit him.

The umbrella stopped the bags and that side of his body abruptly. His momentum brought him around sharply, right over the top rail of the stairs.

"Whoooaaaaaa!" he cried as he went over, slowly somersaulting in the air as he fell. He landed flat on his back on the couch below, bounced completely to his feet, and disappeared through the front door in an out-of-control run. A crashing noise followed his departure.

James and the ladies looked over the rail in wonder. The clerk behind the desk, a customer, and a couple of men walking through the lobby were frozen in their tracks, unable to believe what they had just seen.

"Do you suppose he does that all the time?" Mary Jane asked. "I'm sure it is quite entertaining for the guests, but it seems rather dangerous and foolhardy to me."

The tracks stopped. The final horse Slocum had been following turned into a small homestead and quickly proved to belong to the old man who lived there. Slocum rode back through the melting snow to stare at the unmarked road that stretched out before him.

"I don't get it," he said aloud. "I followed every trail that led off this road. Cleared every one of them. This don't make a lick of sense less'n that old bronc of his has learned to fly."

He turned around. "Nothing to do but go back—it'll be getting dark soon."

They came out of the hotel to find the young porter in a heap under the wagon. James helped him up. "What happened, son?"

The young man was clearly dazed. "Hanged if I know. I was starting down the stairs with the bags, and the next thing I know I'm under this wagon."

James dusted him off. "Well, it was right interesting watching you make the trip. Are you all right?"

"I seem to be."

James stowed the luggage in the wagon and helped Ma up, then gave Mary Jane a hand to the high seat. He climbed up, took the reins in hand, then paused. He had a quizzical look on his face.

"We gonna go or not?" Ma asked.

"Something ain't right."

Mary Jane leaned forward to look under his hat brim. "What is it?"

"I don't know. Ross went this way. The outlaw said so. Slocum is chasing him, only ..."

"Only what?"

"It feels more like he's back behind us."

"Don't be silly. How could he be back behind us?" She smoothed the wrinkles from her skirt and tied her bonnet. She sat there waiting for the wagon to begin to move, then looked back at James, and said, "Well?"

"He's behind us, I tell you. I can feel him strong as ever."

"And I tell you, he can't be. We'll ask John David about it."

"John David? Oh, you mean Slocum. We'll do that if we see him. Say, when did you two get on a first-name basis?"

"I believe that is a first *and* second name, and it is none of your business. We'll see him sooner than you think, because that's him coming down the street."

James had a scowl on his face as he looked up to see the ranger approaching. *None of my business, eh? After we travel halfway across the country together. I've got half a notion to ...* but he dismissed the idea. The last thing he wanted to do was get physical with Bulldog Slocum.

Slocum rode up, tipped his hat to Mary Jane, then leaned inside to acknowledge Ma as well. "Morning, ladies. I see you're ready to pull out, James."

"I was, but I seem to be pointing the wrong direction."

"That so?"

"James said he can feel his brother behind him now," Mary Jane said. "I told him everybody agrees he went south." She punctuated the sentence with a small glance over her shoulder, sticking her nose up in the air.

"I'm with James. I lost his trail down the road a piece. I figure he doubled back and passed the town in the night. He's probably headed back to No Man's

196   TERRY W. BURNS

Land." He laughed. "I imagine he thinks that's the last place I'd look. Might have been too."

She looked confused. "Doubled back? You mean he really ... James did ... I mean, James is right?"

"I ain't laughing at the fact that he can sense his twin anymore, miss, and that's a fact."

"Oh my, I'm sorry I didn't believe you, James."

"No harm done. I'm going to get this rig turned around. You coming with us, *John David?*"

The ranger's eyes narrowed. "How come you say it like that? People don't generally use my first name."

"Mary Jane does. She allowed as how you two are on a first-name basis now."

"First and *second* name," Mary Jane corrected.

James grimaced. Slocum on the other hand looked quite pleased as he said, "That so? Guess I missed when that came about."

"Small wonder, it seems to be a big secret as to exactly when it happened." James pulled the reins hard to the right and flicked the mules with the whip. Begrudgingly they came around. He straightened them back out and walked them out of town, the ranger riding alongside.

"I have to say that Mary Jane and my dear departed mama are the only ones that use that handle on me though." As an afterthought he tipped his hat to the inside of the wagon. "And you, Mrs. Campbell, that goes without saying."

"Thank you, John David," Ma responded.

"Well, you don't have to worry about me," James said. "Slocum seems to fit in my mouth better anyway."

When they got to the wagon yard, they saw that the preacher's wagons were ready to go as well. "We've sure enjoyed traveling with you," Amos said. "I've got a couple of stops to make on our way to Denver. Mind if we trail along until our paths part?"

James smiled. "We'd enjoy that."

Ross came to the Red River, but instead of crossing, he turned to ride upstream beside the river. He pulled up suddenly. *There's that feeling again. Kinda spooky. I keep feeling it, but I don't know what it means. I just feel like ... like ... wait a minute, I know what it feels like. It's James. It's like we're tied together ... connected in some way. Funny, all these years, and that never dawned on me.*

Ross turned around to look back, his hand on the sorrel's rump. *He's turned around. He's coming after me, sure as I'm sitting here. That's bad. That ranger's gonna find out which way they went and follow them right to me. This is no good at all. I'll never shake Slocum if he has that human bloodhound to lead him down my trail.*

Ross turned around and put heels to his horse. *Well, I can make much better time than that wagon can. If Slocum catches up with them, he can't follow his bloodhound and make time too.*

Twenty-six

*S*locum led his horse on a long rein as he and Mary Jane walked together some distance from the wagons. James drove on glumly. "They make a right nice-looking couple, don't they?" Ma observed.

James couldn't believe his ears. "You too, Ma?"

"Now what's that supposed to mean?" She looked at his downcast expression and understood. "I had no idea. How long you had feelings for the girl?"

"Long time, Ma. I had to keep it quiet 'cause she had her cap set for Ross. A man can't cut in on his own brother."

"That's not your brother she's walking with."

"Don't you think I know that?" He turned a shocked expression toward her. "Oh, I'm sorry, Ma. I didn't mean to sass you."

"Just anger talking. How come you haven't declared yourself to her? She can't read minds, you know."

"I nearly done it back in the restaurant at Fort Worth—only she prodded at me, said I was jealous. The next thing I knowed, I was denying it. I don't know why."

Ma's chest moved slightly with suppressed laughter. "I ain't making fun of you, Son. You're just inexperienced in the ways of courting. Reckon that's my fault. We need to talk."

Mary Jane glanced back over at the wagon. James and Ma were talking in an animated fashion, occasionally glancing in the direction of the couple walking together. *I really am wicked teasing James this way, but he really should declare himself if he has any interest.* She stole a glance at the man beside her. *Or do I even want him to? John David is so strong, so dependable. So exciting! There's an air of danger about him.*

Slocum walked along with his hat in his hand. He said little, casual conversation being very difficult for him. "It's nice out," he ventured. The weather was always a safe topic.

"Yes, it is." She could have made it easier for him, but she wasn't sure why she didn't want to. She was determined that she would make one of these two men say something, declare his intentions. He pulled at his collar as if it were choking him.

"You know, Mary Jane, I told you in the restaurant I had feelings for you."

She suppressed a smile. "Yes, John David, just before you went running out the door like your pants were on fire."

He pulled up short and threw his hat on the ground. "Dang it, Mary Jane, how come you keep spurring me? You know what I'm getting at, but you ain't helping any." It was beyond his understanding why she kept making things so hard.

In the wagon, Ma pointed at the exhibition. "Looks like somebody else is getting frustrated."

That observation perked James up. "It does, doesn't it?"

The improvement in his disposition was short lived as the ranger suddenly swept Mary Jane into his arms and kissed her.

"Looks like he found a way around having to talk," Ma said.

Mary Jane stepped back, wide eyed, caught off guard by the sudden move. "Oh my," was all she could muster. Her bonnet dropped from her fingers as she moved away. Slocum thought she was falling and took a quick step to reach for her arm. He missed.

His spur got tangled in the bonnet, and he lost his balance. He fought to keep from going down, losing his grip on the reins and hitting his horse in the face with his hat. The animal was gone in three quick bounds as Slocum lost his battle and fell flat on his back.

"Dang it! Dang it!" He jumped to his feet and ran after the animal. "Come back here, you first cousin to a lop-eared mule."

Running in spurs was not a graceful act, and Slocum's language got much more colorful when he felt he was out of earshot of the ladies. He disappeared over the ridge.

James nearly fell off the seat, laughing. "You shouldn't make fun of the man like that," Ma said, but she was laughing heartily herself.

James shifted the course of the wagon to go pick up Mary Jane. She was red faced as she climbed back up on the seat. "That wasn't the most romantic kiss I ever saw," he volunteered.

Her eyes blazed as she turned on him. "You keep it up, and I'm going to go back and ride with Brother Amos."

"Whoa, I didn't mean to rile you. I reckon you know by now I'm pretty hung up on you myself. You can't blame me for being a little glad things worked out the way they did."

Her eyes softened. "Hung up? That sounds more like you're caught in a fence or a trap than it does something a girl would like to hear."

Ma was right. This girl is gonna play games until she coaxes out what she wants to hear. "Yes, I reckon that wasn't a very genteel way to say it." He swallowed a lump the size of an acorn. There was no way around it. "All right, this is hard, almighty hard. I guess I'm trying to find a way to say I think I love you."

"You think?" There was the coy smile again.

"You want it all, don't you? All right, I *know* I love you. I have for a long time, but I couldn't speak up 'cause you thought you were promised to Ross. It looks like Ross is out of the picture now, so I'm declaring myself." He pulled her to him and gave her a hard kiss.

Holding her in a tight embrace also exerted pressure on the right reins. The two of them stayed locked in the embrace for quite some time before Ma said, "You do know you're aiming the team at that drop-off, don't you?"

James sprang into motion. "Whoa, whoa!" He put his weight into the reins, pulling the mules up short. The wagon passengers looked down. It wasn't a cliff, but it was enough of a drop to have been a real attention-getter had they gone over it.

James looked at Mary Jane curiously. "Kissing you can be dangerous business."

Twenty-seven

Topping the ridge, Slocum saw that the horse had calmed down and was grazing. He walked up to the animal, talking softly, patting him on the neck and stroking his mane. "I'm sorry, fellow. I didn't mean to hit you in the face with my hat. Can't blame you for getting spooked."

He looked back toward the wagon. He couldn't see it; it was over the rise. *Reckon there really is something to Mary Jane being a jinx, the way Ross claims? Things do seem to happen around her.* He put the thought out of his mind. *Naw, I don't believe there is any such thing as a jinx ... Hello, what's this?*

Slocum walked over to a little grove of trees. Someone had camped there. He knelt down and felt the ashes of the fire. *Almost cold, but not completely,* he thought. *It's been the better part of a day since this was burning.*

The ranger walked around the campsite, searching for the place where the horse had been picketed. *That's what I'm looking for. Horseshoe on the left forefoot has a bar on it; that's Campbell's horse for sure. I'll never catch him if I stay with the wagon.* He shook his head, marveling at the fact that James seemed to be piloting his wagon directly toward where Ross had come. *Amazing.*

He stood up and followed the tracks out a ways. *Nice clear trail, easy to follow. I'd best get on it.* He looked back again. *I have to at least let them know I'm going though. What a time! Just when I'm making some headway with Mary Jane.* He mounted his horse and swung it around.

For the first time the ranger felt a conflict between personal interests and the call of duty. It was a new experience for him. He wanted to stay with Mary Jane and see if he could awaken some feelings in her, but he was a man who had always put duty above all else. Even as he rode back to take his leave, he knew he would do it again if the situation arose—which it was bound to do.

He topped the rise to see the wagon coming toward him. A*mazing,* he thought again. *He's not following tracks; he's just riding where his head tells him to ride.*

He rode up to the wagon and looked at James. "I picked up your brother's trail."

James nodded. "I'm not surprised."

"I can't catch up to him and stay with this wagon. I have to get to following those tracks." He reached over to place his large, sun-browned hand over the white, delicate one resting in Mary Jane's lap. "I'm hoping we get to continue our discussion soon."

"You know where I'll be, John David."

"I do for a fact." He smiled and reined the sorrel in a tight circle. Lifting his hat in a salute, he spurred his horse and rode off smartly.

"That was kind of a grandstand play," James said.

"Careful, James, your jealousy is showing again."

"Yes, I know. I can't help it."

She looked at him frankly. *He's admitting it? My, my, how very interesting.*

Ross heard them before he saw them, cows bawling at one another. The magnitude of the hubbub could mean only one thing ... a small trail herd. *Well, well, this ought to disguise my tracks a bit, unless that ranger wants to check out the tracks of every rider going out from the herd after stragglers.*

The chuck wagon was still in place, feeding the night herders, so he aimed toward it. There would be coffee, maybe even a little breakfast. "Hello the camp!" he called, waiting to be invited in.

"Come on in," the cook shouted. "I've got biscuits and gravy these yahoos ain't managed to eat up yet."

"That sounds mighty good."

The old man wiped a hand on the towel he wore for an apron before he extended it. "They call me Spuds. I cook lots of 'taters and beans."

"Campbell, Ross Campbell," he said, leaning over and pumping the cook's hand. "Man could do worse than live on 'taters and beans." Ross stepped down. He tied the horse off to the wagon wheel, on the rear side where there was a little grass within reach.

Spuds put a half-dozen sourdough biscuits on a tin plate and then ladled gravy from an iron skillet over them. He handed it to Ross, then poured him a tin cup full of coffee.

Ross sopped a biscuit in the gravy and took a big bite. "Mmmmmmmm," he muttered. "These wranglers are mighty lucky to be sidling up to grub like this."

Ross knew that cowboys on a drive spent more time rawhiding the cook than they did complimenting the chow, so a generous compliment would bring him all the food he wanted. Besides, what he said was true.

"Thanks, partner. Don't hear good things like that often. This is an ungrateful bunch to sling grub for. Hey, if you've got the room, I've got a little apple pie tucked away. Them jokers don't know it wasn't all ate up."

"Thanks, I'll save room. You guys headed to Dodge?" He looked around the camp—no campfire social going on here. The last nighthawk was stuffing his face as though it might be his last meal. The other two had already turned into their blankets and were probably sound asleep. It was the code of the trail driver: "Eat when you can get it; sleep when there's time."

"Naw, this herd's going to the Double D. Gonna

be breeding stock." The cook was cleaning and packing, getting ready to move to the next campsite.

"That's Waggoner's spread. You know a guy there
name of Mack Steadham?"

"Sure thing." He paused in wiping out some tin
plates he had just fished from a pan of hot, soapy
water. "He's the foreman."

"You tell him I said howdy."

"You must really get around, cowboy."

"Been known to." Ross began to sop up what was
left of the gravy with a biscuit. "Listen, you're likely
to have more company here before long. Fellow by
the name of Slocum." He popped the dripping biscuit
into his mouth.

"Bulldog Slocum? The ranger?" Spuds threw the
wet towel over his shoulder and stowed the dried
pans in the chuck box on the back of the wagon. He
started wiping the lid of the box that folded down to
form his worktable, busy work so he wouldn't have
to maintain eye contact.

"That's him." Ross wiped gravy from his mouth
with his sleeve.

"He after you?"

"A little matter of an unsecured loan from the
bank."

Spuds stopped cleaning to give a belly laugh.
"Shucks, I've known a lot of cowboys get down on
their luck and stand up a bank or maybe have a loose
rope for a cow or two. Just a temporary thing to get
them back on their feet."

Ross brought his plate to the wagon, but instead
of handing it back to Spuds, he dipped it into the

wash pan and cleaned it up himself. The act did not go unnoticed. "Slocum acts like it's a big thing or something."

Seeing Ross wash his plate helped Spuds make up his mind. "I'll tell you what I'll do. I'll keep him so busy eating that he'll lose a bunch of time; then I'll send him off in the wrong direction."

"I'd appreciate that, but I don't want you to do anything that wouldn't set right with you."

"Reckon it's nothing I can't live with."

Ross stood there holding the now-clean plate. "You said something about pie?"

Twenty-eight

Slocum had been riding toward the pinpoint of light for some time. He came up on the herd in the dark, circling wide to keep from spooking them. A night herder waved to him. Adding new words to the song he was singing to keep the cattle calm, he sang about the night camp being over the rise to his left. Slocum already knew that from the light of the fire, but he waved his thanks for the information.

He pulled up to hail the camp and was invited in. Most of the hands were already asleep in their blankets around the fire. He rode over to the chuck wagon.

"That a ranger badge on your chest, stranger?" Spuds asked.

"It is. My name's Slocum." He leaned down and extended a hand, and Spuds shook it.

"Step down, Ranger. You picked a good night to ride the grub line. Ain't often we have steak, but we had one critter take a bad fall today. Bad for the cow," he grinned, "but good for the cowboys. I baked some 'taters and cooked up a mess of red beans to go with it. Apple pie for dessert."

Slocum had been contemplating mooching a cup of coffee and riding on, but this invitation was far too tempting to ride past. "Sure wasn't what I was figuring on doing, but I reckon there are some things you can't ride around."

"A big beefsteak would be pretty hard to pass up, all right."

Spuds handed the ranger a plate completely covered with a huge slab of steak. It had beans and a potato heaped on top of it. Slocum cut a big slice of meat. "Man, this is awful tall eatin'. Lucky cowboys."

"Tell them that." He gestured toward the hands rolled into blankets by the fire. "They don't do nothing but complain."

"Just part of the trail herders' code," he mumbled around a big bite of meat.

"Sure, I know they're just playing around, but sometimes it gets old."

Slocum nodded. "Can see how it would."

"'Course it's rare we get steak. The boss man don't believe in eating his cash crop. The boys are sure happy when one of them breaks a leg or somethin'."

"Sure glad I came along. You grill up a mighty

fine piece of meat." Slocum carved off another large bite and popped it into his mouth. Speaking around it as he chewed, he asked, "You ain't seen a guy by the name of Ross Campbell, have you?"

"He come by early this morning. Said he was on his way to the Waggoner spread. Mentioned some guy by the name of Mack Steadham up there."

Slocum nodded. "I appreciate that. It'll help me make up miles to know where he's heading."

Spuds smiled. He had kept his word. No point in a good cowhand down on his luck having any more trouble than necessary. Still, he felt a little guilty about it. Fortunately he knew how to ease his conscience.

"Any time. You ready for that pie?"

"You sure have been quiet today." James put his plate in the tub of hot water to soak and sat down on the log beside Mary Jane. His mother had already said her good nights and gone to bed.

"I have a lot on my mind," replied Mary Jane. She sat looking at the fire, staring deep into its depths.

A fire can do that to people, drawing them in, mesmerizing them, James thought. He looked at the fire as well. "Am I any part of your thoughts?"

She nodded.

"Don't you think we ought to talk about it?"

She needed to talk, all right, but she wasn't sure James was the person she needed to talk to. He was part of the problem. "I don't know. I'm very confused. I started this trip running after a man I was dead sure was the only man in the world for me.

Now I have serious doubts about that. Then along comes not one, but two men bent on declaring themselves to me. It sweeps a girl off her feet. Yet a part of me is still hitched to Ross, so I suppose I'm being pulled three ways."

"Sorry to hear you aren't more clear on your feelings." *That was lame,* James thought, but it was all he was able to come up with on the spur of the moment. He wasn't very good at this kind of stuff.

She put a hand on his arm and met his eyes. "If you had asked me a while back how it would feel to have men competing for my attention, I would have said it would be wonderful, exciting. It isn't wonderful; it's confusing. My emotions are all jumbled up."

"I don't intend to press you, but I do intend to keep reminding you of my feelings for you."

"How did that come about all of a sudden? For a long time you couldn't even let me know how you feel, and now you can't shut up about it."

"It's not anything new, but I couldn't admit them feelings even to myself while I thought Ross was in the picture. A man don't steal his brother's girl, it just isn't done."

"I see, but why now?"

"It started looking like Ross wasn't in the picture no more. Besides, Ma let me know that if I didn't speak up, I was gonna find myself on the outside looking in. Once I jumped in, I found out the water wasn't as deep and cold as I thought it was." He took her hands and pulled her around to face him.

"I don't want to run anybody down, but Ross ain't got nothing to offer you but misery. Slocum is a good man, probably better than me, but all he's got in the world is on that horse with him. And that badge on his chest is more than an ornament; it's his life. Every time it calls, he's gonna go. He could have stayed here and made his play for you, but he didn't. He followed that badge to find Ross."

She measured the sincerity on his face and didn't find it lacking. She had been having many of the same thoughts. "My head knows that what you're saying is true, but sometimes hearts don't listen."

"You just remember this: I may not have any more in this world than they do, but someday soon this wagon is going to stop moving, and when it does, I'll put down roots. I'll sink 'em right there, and I'll sink 'em deep. You'll never have to wonder where I am or what I'm doing, 'cause I'll be right by your side—that is, if you decide to stay there with me."

Slocum didn't have to waste time tracking now. He knew where Ross was going. He took a more direct line that would cut hours off the ride. He rode at a pace that ate up miles without tiring his mount any more than necessary. This more relaxed ride freed up his mind to think, and his thoughts were on Mary Jane.

This is dumb. What's one more outlaw in the grand scheme of things? If I catch up to him and kill him, she's liable to hate me for it. If I catch up to him and bring him back alive, she's likely to remember she's hung up on him and pay me no never mind. My best play would have been to stay there and go to courting her proper like. But here I am, riding along after the man she's been pining for and following after for months, like I don't have good sense. If I did have good sense, I'd turn around right now and go back and try to set things right.

But he didn't turn around. He continued to berate himself about how big a mistake he was making, but it wasn't in him to let personal feelings interfere with his duty as a lawman. He had never quit on a man once he went after him, and he couldn't do it now. He wanted to, but he just couldn't.

It was after noon on the third day when Slocum rode into the Waggoner Ranch headquarters. Steadman and a half-dozen cowboys sat on the porch of the cookhouse, drinking coffee. He rode up to them.

"Howdy, Ranger. Care to join us?"

"Hello, Mack. You seen Ross Campbell?"

"You still looking for him? No wonder they call you Bulldog. No, I ain't seen him since the last time you asked."

"But I was told that ..." Suddenly it dawned on him. When was he going to learn how Campbell used that good-natured manner of his to cajole people into helping him? He realized that either he had been suckered, or he was being suckered right now. He looked around the group. No, one of them would be sure to say so if that were the case. The guilty party in this wild-goose chase had to be the cook. *I've got half a notion to go back and put some lumps the size of goose eggs all over that old man's head.*

Twenty-nine

Jacksboro turned out to be a collection of ram-shackle buildings, but it did have both a schoolhouse and a church. *A sure sign of progress,* Ross thought as he tied up his horse in front of the saloon. He pushed through the batwing doors and stood there a moment to get accustomed to the light. He was surprised to see a number of soldiers among the clientele.

Ross moved to the bar to take a place beside a beefy sergeant. "Didn't know there was any military around here," he commented.

"Aye, lad, that there is, the Fourth Calvary under the command of Col. Ranald S. Mackenzie." He brought himself to a shaky semblance of attention, saluted, then slouched back onto the bar. "We're buildin' a stone fort outside of town called Fort Richardson."

"That kind of work could build a powerful thirst in a man, all right."

"It does indeed." He punctuated the sentence with a prodigious gulp from the mug in front of him, raining half its contents at once. He wiped his mouth, then grabbed Ross by the shirtfront, pulled him close, and confided in him. His breath would have peeled varnish off a good table. "I ought to be out leading a squad in some fine military action, instead I get to lead all these fine young misfits"—he included all the soldiers in the room with an expansive gesture—"back to the fort to pile rocks until they add up to a buildin'."

He let go of Ross and turned back to the bar before adding, "What kind of work is that for a fightin' man, I ask you?"

"A waste," Ross said, the man's breath eliminating the need to purchase another drink. He patted the burly man on the back. "Well, you're a fount of information, Sergeant." Ross turned and leaned back against the bar. The card games were mostly made up of soldiers. *Not worth the effort, those guys get paid once a month and don't see enough money even then to fund one good outing in town. These would be penny-ante games with very sparing pots. I'd rather get a good night's sleep and be on my way early tomorrow morning.*

The sergeant saw where he was looking. "Fancy a game?"

"Not much of a card player. I think I'll pass."

"Pity. Some of the boys are sportin' their reenlistment bonus. They'd not be adverse to runnin' it up a bit."

"Reenlistment bonus? You don't say. Well, I suppose if I can help the cause a bit, it'd be a small enough repayment for all they do." *And a professional gambler up against a bunch of drunken soldiers should make for easy pickings.*

As it turned out, they were drunk enough not to notice how much he was taking them for, but they *weren't* drunk enough to fail to do something about it when it finally dawned on them. The corporal next to him accused him of cheating and jumped to his feet. Ross had him covered with a gun before he could move, but a watching soldier then broke a chair over Ross's head. He crumpled where he stood and didn't get up.

In a rage, and robbed of the intended target for that rage, the remaining soldiers did the only thing they could do according to their code—they turned on each other.

Ross awoke the next morning in a cell full of soldiers. "What happened?"

A soldier gave him a wry smile. "We chose up partners and had a little dance, but you missed most of it."

Ross rubbed his aching head. "Where's my money?"

"The first sergeant has it. Except for what you had on the table. That went to pay for the damage."

"Figures. How do I get out of here?"

"We've already had to face the colonel. Being a civilian, you'll be taken over to stand in front of the county judge, whenever they get around to it."

"Oh great." Ross hoped it wouldn't take long. He was losing whatever lead he had managed to build up. If Slocum had bitten on the red herring he had laid down about the Waggoner Ranch, it wouldn't buy him much time, if any. If Slocum hadn't gone for it, he was likely to walk in the jail any minute. Ross was trying to clear his aching head when the conversation across the guardhouse drew his attention:

"Gold, you say?" A corporal was quizzing a private lying on a cot. The private's shirt was faded except for the place where sergeant's stripes had previously been sewn.

"Over in New Mexico Territory. A place just up in the mountains they call Elizabethtown. There's a lot of men getting rich up there."

The curly-headed corporal nodded knowingly. "You deserted to go after it?"

"I was only gone for a while. I figured to rake in some gold, cash it in and get rich, and then come back. I knew I'd lose my stripes, but I figured it'd be worth it."

"But it didn't work out?"

"It never does," the sergeant-turned-private said bitterly.

"Where are we headed?" Ma rocked her chair forward to peek out at James.

He leaned over to be heard better, but he didn't take his eyes off what passed for a road. One unobserved large stone, and he could find himself trying to change a wheel with little in the way of tools. "I'm told the nearest town is Jacksboro. There's a cavalry post there."

Her determination had not wavered. "You think Ross came this way?"

"Sure feels like it to me."

She nodded, absorbing the information. "When you figure us to get there?"

"Late tomorrow, maybe the day after. Mary Jane still asleep?"

Ma glanced over at the form on the bed beside her. "Dead to the world. Good thing too—she hasn't been sleeping at night. Has too much on her mind."

James snorted. "If she'd just listen to me, she wouldn't have that much on her mind."

"You're doing well not pressing her. She needs time to think on it. Although thinking about such a thing can be a lot like a puppy chasing its tail, going round and round and not getting anywhere at all."

"I don't understand why it's not clear to her."

"That's because you think the logic is all on your side. You figure you're the safest bet, and you are. The problem is, she doesn't know who it is she actually loves." *Men*, she thought. But it couldn't be dismissed that easily—this was not just any man— this was her firstborn son, by almost two minutes.

"You think love has anything to do with it?"

"It has everything to do with it, Son. Everything."

James straightened back up, shaking his head. Things were so confusing. Inside the wagon, speaking softly so he wouldn't hear, Mary Jane roused and in a sleepy voice said, "Was he just talking about me?"

Ma didn't look up but continued to work on the needlepoint in her lap. "Maybe. Why?"

Mary Jane scooted over to sit beside Ma, turning her back to James to make it harder to be overheard. "I don't know what to do, Ma. I like all three of them."

"Sure you do," Ma clucked, "but I didn't hear the word *love* in there anywhere."

Mary Jane fingered the needlepoint in Ma's lap as if she were inspecting it. "I'm not even sure I know what that is. I was sure I loved Ross. Now I don't know."

"When we're young, we expect love to be like a blazing fire," Ma said with a fond smile. "I expect my man and I were on fire a few times. But that's just the physical. Real love is not a feeling—it's an action. It's wanting to be together all the time and being comfortable with one another. It's finishing each other's sentences and caring more about what the other person wants than what you want. It's figuring out that you are two halves that together make a whole. The fire is nice, and necessary, but it's the other that makes it all work."

"So you're telling me I should choose James?"

Ma looked over the top of her sewing glasses at her. "Why do you say that? I didn't point you at anybody. Are you saying you feel that way about him?"

Mary Jane hugged her knees to her chest. "We're good together, I know that. Is he the one? I don't know."

"Why don't you talk to Brother Amos about it, dear? He might be quite a help."

"Maybe I will."

Thirty

*B*ack on the trail, Slocum pondered his next move. If Ross hadn't come through here on his way back to Indian Territory or up to No Man's Land, it meant he had doubled back again and was headed south to Mexico or west to New Mexico Territory. If it was west, he had probably taken the road through Jacksboro or the more southerly route through Fort Stockton. He resolved to check Jacksboro first, and if he had no luck there, he would wire the rangers down on the border to intercept Ross as he hotfooted it southwestward to Fort Stockton.

It sounded like a workable plan, and he put hard heels to his horse. Knowing the capacity of the animal, he would have to make the best time possible in order to catch up. As Ross had feared, Slocum was eating up the lead the gunman had gained before being thrown in the military cell.

When the ranger rode into Jacksboro, he quickly learned that he had missed his quarry by less than a day. "He rode out this morning?" he said to the grizzled first sergeant. "Just my luck. It couldn't have been as easy as me coming in, putting cuffs on him right in that cell, and toting him back."

The burly sergeant pulled the pipe from his mouth and said, "In all my years, I can't remember a time I 'got anything the easy way."

"Yeah, you're right there. You have any idea where he was headed?"

"Rode out westerly is all I know," said Sergeant O'Donnell. "There's a couple of boys over muckin' out stalls that shared a cell with him for a while. They might know somethin'."

The sergeant got up, put his pancake cavalry hat on his head, and tucked the strap under his chin. He sucked in his big belly, tucked his riding crop under his arm, and led Slocum out the door.

He was like a bear crossing the parade ground, speaking to first one soldier and then another. "Johnson, what are you lazin' around on the porch for? Haven't you got things to do? I can find somethin' if you don't!" He scowled as the private scurried for cover. Slocum could see that O'Donnell lived for this.

O'Donnell's gaze swung to another trooper tying a horse to the hitching rail. "Donovan, loosen the cinch on that horse until you're ready to ride out.

How would you like it if I tied a rope around your belly so tight you could barely breathe, then left you standin' in the hot sun!" The first sergeant seemed to have no volume under a roar.

When they entered the stable, the tone of the big man changed from the familiar, chiding one. It was obvious that he and the man he addressed had been friends for many years. "Private Muldoon, could I be after havin' a moment of your time?"

"Aye, First Sergeant. Takin' a break would be to me taste." He moved closer. "And have you heard the colonel talk of me? Is he thinkin' court-martial or just a wee bit of post discipline?"

"Am I expected to be able to read minds now?" O'Donnell focused on something far off in the distance, rocking back and forth on his heels, hands behind his back.

"Oh, come on, Seamus. We've soldiered together too long for you to be actin' all high and mighty. Sure, and have you not spoken up for me a'tall?"

O'Donnell glanced at Muldoon out of the corner of his eye and softened. He turned to his friend and laid a hand on his shoulder. "You know I have, lad. I think the colonel will make an example of you for a while, but I expect you'll be wearin' your stripes again soon. You're too good a man not to. It was a fool thing to do though."

Muldoon looked properly contrite as he admitted his shortcoming. "Gold can do funny things to a man."

"Gold?" Slocum spoke up. They seemed to notice him for the first time.

"Gold it is," Muldoon said. "Like a fool I went chasin' after it."

Slocum smiled. "Unless I miss my guess, I don't need to ask you if Campbell headed that way."

"Ross? He didn't say, but he was most interested in my story about what was happenin' over at Elizabethtown, in New Mexico Territory."

Slocum's eyes bored into the man. "Where is that?"

"You can't miss it. You go up Cimarron Canyon, then follow the stream back west when you reach the valley at the top."

"I'll do just that, and I hope you get those stripes back."

"I'm a-thankin' you. I hope so meself."

First Sergeant O'Donnell sucked in his belly and stuck out his chest. "Now, *Private*, if you are quite through, it appears you have a number of stalls to go yet."

"Aw, Seamus, have a heart."

"It's a heart you're wantin', is it? If I had no heart I'd be in there doin' me duty—beggin' the colonel to have you up on charges for bein' such a bad example to the lads. You should be grateful that I haven't done it."

Slocum could see that this conversation was not going to end anytime soon, so he quietly took his leave. He had a long ride ahead of him.

Slocum had missed Ross by less than a day, and the small wagon train pulled in the following day, missing Slocum by almost the same margin. The ladies stayed in the wagon as James went into the sutler's store to see what he could find out. Stretching their legs, the three from the other wagon came up to see what was going on.

"James is checking to see if his brother has been here," Ma explained. "Then we'll decide what we want to do."

The man James chose to ask was one Sean Muldoon, wearing a brand-new set of corporal's stripes that fell short of covering the faded spot left by the three sergeant's stripes he had earlier worn.

"Ross Campbell?" Muldoon eyed the man. "You wouldn't be funnin' me, would you?" Why would this man come back to town pretending to be someone else. He knew a trick when he saw one.

James understood and laughed. "I know, I know, you think I'm him, but I'm his twin brother, James."

"If you be not him, 'tis a twin you are indeed. Well now, ain't that a caution? Aye, I spent some time with him." He leaned over, lowering his voice to add, "In the guardhouse it was."

James adopted the conspiratorial tone as well. "He was in trouble?"

"Oh, nuthin' serious. He's a right popular man, your brother; there was another fella here yesterday lookin' for him."

"A Texas Ranger?"

That question took the corporal aback. "He didn't say."

"Wiry little man, black hair and mustache?"

"Aye, that's him. They went west from here."

"How do you know that?"

"Ross is headed up to the gold fields at Elizabethtown, in New Mexico Territory. The other fella took out after him."

James thanked the corporal and then went out to report to the others. He found them talking to a distinguished-looking officer who introduced himself as Colonel Ranald S. Mackenzie. "The colonel has asked us to share his table with him this evening," Ma announced.

James shook the man's hand, then looked at her. "It's early, Ma. You sure you don't want to follow up on this lead? It's the closest we've been to Ross in some time."

"I'm afraid I must insist," the colonel said. "It is rare that we get the company of such charming ladies out here, and my wife would never forgive me if I failed to bring them home. And that's not to mention the presence of a man of the cloth. I can't remember the last time a minister came through, though we do have a chaplain on the post who conducts services."

James gave in to the wishes of the others. It proved to be a most pleasant evening, and the food was excellent. Following the meal, First Sergeant O'Donnell marched four troopers into the room. He removed his cap, looked at the colonel's lady, and said, "With your kind permission, ma'am, the regimental singers would like to offer you a bit of entertainment."

Mrs. Mackenzie nodded her permission, and the first sergeant stepped to the side, snapped to attention, and winked at the men. They launched into a medley of songs, in tight, impeccable four-part harmony.

When they had finished, the first sergeant gave the command, "Left face, forward march," and the soldiers began to march out, to the applause of those assembled. They were through the door and onto the porch when the first sergeant turned slightly to doff his cap and say, "Ladies," as he exited.

The maneuver caused him to turn toward the chest on top of which the ladies' wraps and Mary Jane's umbrella lay. The crook of the umbrella handle became ensnared around the ankle of the unsuspecting O'Donnell, sending him headlong down the front steps. It was like watching dominoes topple as all the men went down in a heap.

"Here now," the colonel said, rising from his chair. "What's all this?"

The men scrambled to their feet and stood at attention. The colonel closed on them, employing his command voice. "Have you men already drunk your liquor ration and just before coming to present yourselves to a group of ladies?"

O'Donnell flushed red and looked as if he had a ramrod jammed down his back. "No sir, we'd never do such a thing. It was just clumsy of me, sir. I got me feet tangled up."

"Very well, Sergeant. Just be more careful in the future. Good job, men. We are greatly appreciative, in spite of your rather unorthodox exit."

Thirty-one

Ross found the ride across the rolling plains quite relaxing, and the view of the mountain range in the distance was beautiful—the peaks were snow-capped, even though spring was already beginning to show its head in the valleys below. It seemed to take forever to reach the mountains, after which he turned north along the creek, following it to the place where it came down out of Cimarron Canyon.

The land through the canyon was the most beautiful Ross had ever seen. Snow-tipped evergreens on either side of a sparkling stream were just waking up from their winter nap. Here and there rock outcroppings stood in magnificent splendor, some standing as tall as a castle wall.

He followed the stream through the valley until he found the tent city that was Elizabethtown, named for the beautiful daughter of a local miner. It was a bustling place, and the sound of shovels and picks echoed up and down the creek. Here and there sluice boxes emptied the clear water back into the stream, and tents dotted both sides. Everywhere he looked, men squatted by the water, washing gold in pans—it looked like backbreaking work.

Ross wasn't really keen on wielding a pick and shovel, even with gold as the prize for the effort. There had to be an easier way to acquire the magical dust.

He made his way down the row of tents that seemed to delineate the main street until he found one marked "Saloon." There he stopped and dismounted, tied his horse to the hitching post, and went in. The place was deserted except for a couple of old men and a bartender. Obviously everyone was out working the claims.

Ross looked at the bartender. "The owner in?"

The man snickered. "I'm the owner. Name's Bill Slade. You don't think I'd pay somebody to be in this place during the hours it ain't making no money, do you?"

"You got a point there. Gimme a beer." The man slid a full mug to him on the bar. Ross took a long, slow draw, then wiped the foam from his mouth with his sleeve.

"You wanted something else?" The man leaned both forearms on the bar.

"I'm a gambler. You run a house game in here?"

"From time to time. Got nobody dealing right now—you want to run a table? House cut is fifteen percent."

Ross smiled. "Sounds easier to me than grubbing around in the dirt like a gopher."

Slade seemed to understand that logic. "That's why I'm in here."

"How about a place to stay?"

"I've got cots in the back. The night shift is pretty crowded, but I can cut you a good deal on one if you want to sleep days."

"Days will work if I'm playing cards nights. Matter of fact, I could use a nap right now if I'm going to play tonight. Do I get fresh sheets?"

"Sheets?"

"Never mind."

Four hours later Slocum rode into town. He too made straight for the saloon. By the time he arrived, business had picked up a bit, but it was still short of the crowd that would hit after the sun went down. He stepped up to the bar and ordered a drink, then asked the bartender if he'd seen a man fitting the description of Ross Campbell.

"I just come on duty. You might ask the boss. That's him over there. Name is Slade."

Slocum carried his mug with him and walked up to the table. "You Slade?"

"Bill Slade." He nodded to the chair next to him, and Slocum took it. "Somethin' I can do for you?"

"I'm looking for a man." Slocum again went through the description.

"Haven't seen him." Slade held up his mug to signal the bartender for a refill. The bartender refilled it and slid it down the bar to him. Slade reached for it without giving it his full attention, missed it, and it fell and broke. "Man," he said. "I get enough breakage in here; I hate to do it to myself."

The sound of the breaking glass startled Ross awake. He stepped through the curtain into the saloon, backing out quickly when he saw Slocum. He pulled his pistol from the holster and eased the barrel out to shoot the ranger where he sat.

Seeing him, Slade got up to step into in his line of fire. Behind the ranger's back he made a violent motion for Ross to go out the back way. It was clear he wanted no such trouble in his place.

Cursing under his breath, Ross did as Slade had indicated. Once outside, he eased around the saloon, untied his horse, and led it up into the trees. So much for making money playing cards. Even if the ranger rode on, Slade would not be interested in a wanted man dealing cards for him. He tied off the animal high on the ridge overlooking the camp. He needed a new plan.

Ross sat there thinking, watching the camp come alive. The noise level slowly increased, until it hit a fever pitch about midnight. He knew from experience that the raucous prospectors would start to stagger home soon, but that some diehards would last until the morning light. Still others would go crawl into rented cots like the one he had just vacated.

Falling into bed? Maybe there's an even easier way

to get my hands on that dust. He led his horse well down the creek and waited. He let a number of drunken miners pass because the pokes on their belts looked pretty flat. He finally settled on two old geezers who looked to be packing pretty fat pokes. He pulled his bandanna over his face and stepped out, pistol in hand.

"Oh, not again," said one of them, an old man with a flowing white beard.

"Again?" Ross didn't understand.

"Happens right regular around here. Don't worry, we ain't gonna be no trouble. We can always get more gold, but another hide is pretty hard to come by."

"That's very sensible."

"Ask him how he wants to play it, Zeke," the other old man said, showing toothless gums in a humorless grin.

"Good idea, Rufus. We don't want the man to think we ain't cooperative. Somebody else will probably rob him before he gets very far anyway."

Ross wasn't amused. "Toss those pistols in the creek, one at a time, and use your left hands."

"I'm left-handed. That go for me, too?" Zeke said.

"I don't care which hand you use, just throw it."

They did as he asked, but Zeke said, "That ain't right. If you're gonna do a professional job, you ought not talk thataway. Guess you want these pokes now?"

"I hate getting robbed by amateurs," Rufus added. "It's demeaning."

Zeke shook his head. "You and your two-dollar words."

"You boys want to keep your mind on what we're doing here? Toss them pokes."

Zeke raised his hands, then let them fall. "There you go again. You ain't doing a very good job of this. You want we should toss them together or one at a time?"

"Maybe I ought to give you this gun and let you do the robbing; you seem to know so much about it."

Zeke held out a hand for the gun. "Bet your boots I do, and I'd be glad to show you how it oughta be done."

"I think I'll just bumble through on my own." He tossed a pegging string to Rufus. "Tie Zeke up, and tie him tight."

Rufus complied, then stepped back so Ross could test the knots. But Ross paid a little too much attention to the inspection, and Rufus jumped him. Ross laid him out with the barrel of his pistol, but his bandanna was pulled down in the process.

They saw me. He cocked the pistol and contemplated finishing them off. He realized the noise would bring miners running from everywhere. And it wasn't like the ranger couldn't give them a full description anyway. He found an old bandanna in the pocket of the unconscious man and used it to gag Zeke.

With Zeke walking ahead at gunpoint, Ross hauled Rufus into their tent to get him off the trail and to give him more time before they were found.

"While I'm at it, I might as well have a look around." Ross started going through things, looking in containers and jars, but he found nothing of interest. "Looks like those pokes were all you had, eh?"

Zeke nodded enthusiastically.

"You seem a mite too agreeable. There's still something here, isn't there?"

Zeke shook his head vigorously.

"You can't fool me, you old coot. I know you're hiding something."

Zeke shook his head again, mumbling something beneath the gag. He stole a quick glance across the room.

"What was that? What were you looking at? It was over here." Ross walked across the plank floor of the tent. He didn't see anything, but he knew it had to be there. He took a step, and a board squeaked beneath his foot. "Aha, what have we here?"

All the boards were firmly nailed down, except for the one he was looking at now. It was small and had just been laid in position. He drew his knife and pried it up. He glanced over at Zeke and smiled. Zeke rolled his eyes.

Nestled in the crevice below were two bags. Ross pulled one out and untied the string. He struck a match and looked inside. The dust in the bag glistened, reflecting the light of the match. Ross whistled—he was a rich man.

Thirty-two

*T*his is absolutely breathtaking." Mary Jane was spellbound as the trio made their way up Cimarron Canyon. All three of them were crowded into the wagon seat where they had a better view. Compared to the hills and mountains back home, this land was huge, untamed, overwhelming. The fast-moving stream ran by them, laughing and gurgling like a happy child.

"Stop! Stop!" Ma slapped James on the back several times until he reined the team in.

"What is it?"

"Let me out of here, I've had about all of the back of this wagon I can stand."

"But I thought?"

"Trees, mountains, it's wonderful, and smell that air. I want to walk awhile. It'll lighten the load for the team too."

James grinned. Ma walked for a good while. She was in her element, happy as a child coming home. She finally tired and got back into the wagon.

Behind them they could hear loud expressions of awe coming from the other wagons.

"Reminds me of home," James said, "only bigger and better."

"I was thinking the same thing," Ma admitted.

"It's not enough bigger that it causes you a problem?"

"Not in the least."

Farther upstream they met a man named Walker who had settled in an offshoot of the canyon. Amos walked up to see what he had to say. "There's a number of settlers in this canyon," the man said.

"Is settling allowed here?" James asked.

"We're doing it. There's a lot of folderol about some old Spanish and Mexican land grants, so I don't know if our claims will hold up or not, but we're all inclined to give it a shot."

"Hope it works out for you. What's up ahead of us?"

The man pointed. "When you top out the canyon, you can go left or right. Right takes you to a mining town, Elizabethtown. Left will take you around to another canyon leading down to Taos. Were it me, I wouldn't take no decent womenfolk into that there mining town."

"What is Taos?"

"It's a real old town, founded by the Spaniards back in 1400 or 1500 or such. Still lots of Mexicans living there, but there are lots of white folks too."

After a brief visit, the man went on his way.

Amos had walked up to listen to the man as well. After he left, Ma looked out at the two men and said, "It was kinda in my mind that settling here might be something to think on, but not if there's gonna be a fight over land grants."

"I was thinking the same thing, Ma," James said. "I want to get us some land, but I don't want it if we can't get clear title to it. But we have to find someplace we can settle for free, 'cause we sure don't have enough money to buy any land."

"You're right."

"You going to this Taos place?" Amos asked.

"Sounds sensible to me. How about you?"

Amos pondered the question for a couple of moments before responding. "If I turn north and go through Elizabethtown, it'd be a shorter way to Denver, but somehow I feel that stringing along with you a little longer is the right thing to do."

James smiled. "Good, we enjoy having you with us. Let's go see what this Taos place looks like."

Ross didn't run for it. He led his horse into the creek, then back into town. There he mixed his tracks with those on the street and slipped back up on the ridge where he had waited before. As he passed the saloon, he peeked in to see Slocum halfway through a steak the size of a barrelhead. He would be there a while yet.

Back on his perch, Ross dozed off. He was awak-
ened in the early hours of the morning by a
commotion down below. He watched with interest as
the two old men he had robbed came up to the
saloon with a group of men, just as Slocum was coming out of it.

"We hear tell you're a Texas Ranger," Zeke said to
him.

Slocum admitted he was. "We been robbed. I was
tied up, and Rufus got pistol-whipped. Show him,
Rufus."

The old man pulled off his hat and revealed the
fresh bandage on his head. "He got our pokes,
Ranger, but even worse he searched our place and
got our stash as well. That was a couple of months'
work."

Slocum repeated what he had been told ever
since he had left the state of Texas. "Everybody keeps
reminding me that my badge ain't no good over here.
Now all of a sudden everybody wants me to be a lawman. Ain't life funny? Well, what'd this feller look
like?"

"Tall and lanky, with sandy hair, wore a pair of
matched pistols," Zeke said. "Had eyes like you was
looking right through his head at the sky."

Slocum nodded. "That's Campbell. That's the
man I'm here after."

"He was in my place earlier," Slade admitted.
"Wanted to run a table."

Slocum spun around. "I thought you said you
hadn't seen him?"

Slade looked sheepish. "Don't go riding

roughshod over me, Ranger. I didn't know what you wanted him for. I ain't got nobody dealing a game right now."

"What are you going to do, Ranger?" Zeke was in no mood for social conversation.

"I'll try to pick up his track come first light. I intend to go fetch him up."

Zeke rubbed his chin. "Well, if he went back down Cimarron Canyon, we'll soon know it, 'cause he can't get past them settlers without them knowing. If he didn't go that way, he's pretty much got to be going up into Colorado or down toward Taos. I'm betting on Taos, but if that ain't it, you'll have to chase him to Colorado alone. Nobody is going to be willing to be gone from the claims that long. If they're unattended for two weeks, according to mining law, they become abandoned, and somebody will grab them up."

"I didn't figure on anybody riding with me anyway." Slocum gave him a hard look. "I work alone."

"Nobody asked you for permission. It's our dust he got." Zeke matched his hard look. "With you or without you, we're riding after our money. Like you said, that badge don't cut no ice here, and according to mining law, we're the constituted authority in these parts."

Slocum sighed. "All right, I guess I'd rather know where you were and what you were doing."

Ross had watched them through the whole discussion. It was an animated group, arms waving guns, fingers pointing first one way and then the other. It didn't matter which way they decided to go,

Ross would keep them in sight—his greatest safety was in knowing where they were at all times.

The posse turned out to be a dozen men. They mounted up, then headed back down toward Cimarron Canyon.

Ross watched from the top of the ridge as they rode back down, quizzed some settlers, then turned their horses toward Taos. It was going exactly as planned. A couple of hours later he watched as they caught up with James's wagon. "Would you look at that?" he said out loud. "That fool brother is on my trail like a bloodhound, and that ranger knows he can follow it with him. I've got to get him sidetracked. And that silly preacher is still with them. I don't believe it."

Down below, Slocum rode up beside the wagon. "Hello, Mary Jane. Folks."

"Well, John David, where did you come from?" She looked down and began to pat the curls at the base of her neck in an unconscious preening gesture.

"Here and there, yonder and back. Still on the trail." He looked at James. "You still feeling your brother?"

James instinctively looked right at the ridge where Ross sat watching and listening. "He's somewhere nearby," he said. "Seems to be in this general direction, but I'm not sure about this town up ahead. It's downright confusing. Probably 'cause of the way these trails twist all around up here."

"Well, I still gotta say it beats anything I ever saw," Slocum admitted. He turned his attention back to Mary Jane. "You been thinking about what we were talking about?"

"That—and a lot more." *Men! Why would he ask me a thing like that right in front of James?*

"What does that mean?'

She stiffened up. "It means this is not really the time or place to talk about it."

"Oh ... of course." The other riders crowded in on him. "I've got to ride on ahead," he explained. "These boys are getting impatient." He spurred his horse and waved as they rode off.

Ross wanted to ride down and say hello to his family, but until he lost that hellhound ranger and the posse he was leading, he couldn't take that chance. He had to keep an eye on them.

As the posse came out of the canyon, they saw the village of Taos laid out on the valley floor, a collection of square adobe buildings. A short distance beyond was the Indian pueblo. Taos was actually two cities right next to each other, sharing the same valley.

Ross stayed up on the hill, watching the group through a spyglass as they spread out to question residents, but to no avail. They decided to take the quest to the saloon, where the subject was intensely discussed for a couple of hours before the posse mounted up to return to Elizabethtown. Slocum was left alone to pursue the chase up into Colorado.

The ranger sat quietly in the corner of the room after the others had left. He didn't want to go that far north, but what could he do?

"You Slocum?"

He was slipping. He hadn't even been aware the

man had approached the table. Such lack of attention
was dangerous in his business. Slocum nodded to the
question.

"I'm the station agent for Sanderson's Overland
Stage Company. This here message come for you a
couple of days ago."

"No way anybody could know I was going to be
here. I didn't even know myself." He took the folded
paper.

"None of my affair. I just know they sent it all
over the place and figured you'd get it at one place
or t'other." The man turned and walked out. The
message was an order from Texas Ranger headquarters in Waco. He was being recalled. The ranger
detachment was being formed and would move in
force against border raiders.

He got up wearily. No choice but to go. He would
stop and tell Mary Jane good-bye on the way back
down the canyon.

Ross watched him ride out of the valley and back
up the canyon. It made no sense. Bulldog Slocum
never gave up on a scent. But he knew Slocum
would go back to the wagon to see Mary Jane, so that
should give him time to do what he needed to do.

Thirty-three

Ross rode into Taos and headed straight to the saloon, where he bought a couple of drinks for people and learned that Slocum had rushed out right after talking with the station agent. A quick visit to the express office confirmed that Slocum had received a message from Texas Ranger headquarters, the contents of which were unknown.

He'll be back, Ross thought as he left the office. But he felt he had time to conduct some business before that happened. He made his way over to the bank where he made the acquaintance of a distinguished-looking Spanish gentleman by the name of Rafael Montoya. It turned out that Montoya had just what Ross was looking for: eighty acres of land backed up to the mountains, with a good water supply and an existing four-room adobe hacienda. Perfect. And the banker guaranteed that the title could not be disputed.

Ross purchased the property with the gold dust, then gave the banker instructions to deliver the title to a man who would arrive shortly in a wagon with two female companions. "You can't miss him," he said. "He looks just like me, but he will be dressed like a farmer."

The wagon wound its way down the trail along the stream. It was a long pull as the canyon twisted this way and that, making its relentless way toward Taos.

As he rode to meet it, Slocum rehearsed his words over and over: "Mary Jane, you know how much I care for you, but I've been called to duty back in Texas, and I've got to go."

No, that wasn't right. "Mary Jane, I wish I could take you with me, but ..."

No, that was even worse.

He saw the wagon ahead of him and waved with his hat. He rode up to it, and all of the tenderness he wanted to show disappeared. He just couldn't let people see past his bold exterior; it wasn't in him to let down his guard that way. "I've been called back to Austin," he announced. "I have to go."

He pulled off his hat and looked at Mary Jane. He spurred his horse forward a few steps so he could take her hand. He looked at her, running the various phrases through his brain. He knew he had to say something, but all that came out was,

"I'll be coming back."

She smiled sweetly. "That's nice, John David. I fear I'll be worried about you."

"Don't fret none. I'll be all right." He leaned over to kiss her, but at the last moment she turned to offer her cheek to him. He kissed the soft check, then pulled back, puzzlement in his eyes.

"Take care of yourself, John David." She pulled free of his hand and clasped her own hands in her lap.

John David thought, *You fool, you've ridden away too many times. You do it again now, and it won't matter whether you come back or not.* His heart became a lump in his chest. He had to go. He sat there, torn between the conflicting emotions raging inside him. He let none of them show on his face. He never did.

"I have to get going; the captain will skin me alive." He spun his horse and rode off. He stopped at the top of the ridge and waved good-bye. He sensed that this parting would be their last.

As the trio looked at the figure on the top of the ridge, James said, "Hope he's gonna be all right. I hear tell there's some pretty fierce fighting going on down on the border."

Mary Jane watched Slocum wave, then disappear over the ridge. "Yes, I'd hate to see anything happen to him." Sadness welled up inside her. It seemed she was always watching him go. That thought played again in her mind. *That's it, isn't it? He'll always go. When duty calls, he'll always go.*

It was fairly early in the morning when they made Taos. Ma and Mary Jane were oohing and aahing as they drove slowly into the village. It was neat and clean, the pink adobe of the buildings made even rosier by the morning sun.

The wagons pulled to a halt, and Ma and Mary Jane waited for Judy to rush up; then the three of them went into the general store, eager to sample the shopping. Amos helped Joseph down as James stepped over to the saloon to see what he could find out. As he entered, he met two old men coming out. He stepped back to let them pass and wondered at their shocked expressions as they rushed off.

He shook his head and went inside. He asked the bartender about Ross. The man smirked and said, "Yeah, like you wasn't here. You don't even remember? Man, you must have really tied on a good one."

James started to set him straight, but the man moved down to wait on another customer. The homing instinct was still working strong. He drained his drink and rushed back to tell the women.

He entered the store, nearly tripping over two clerks cleaning up some sort of spill on the floor. He walked over to where Ma and Mary Jane were examining some yard goods. "What happened?" He indicated the clerks with a jerk of his thumb over his shoulder.

"Who knows?" Mary Jane said. "It is my experience that people who work in these places tend to be inordinately clumsy."

"Well, Ross has been here, all right. Not more than a day or so ago."

Ma sighed. "He's gone, I take it?"

"I'm afraid so."

He studied her face. All of a sudden, she looked tired. It just came over her as if she had finally resigned herself to the truth. "We'll never catch up to him, trying to chase him on horseback with us in a wagon."

James had known that from the beginning and had tried to say so on a couple of occasions, but she hadn't been ready to hear it. She was ready now, but it wasn't in him to say I told you so. "What are you trying to say, Ma?"

"We need to talk about settling down. We can't keep this up. He knows we're trying to catch up with him, and he knows where we are."

James shook his head. "We don't know that."

"Of course we do. If you can feel him, he can feel you."

"How about if we make camp outside of town on the stream? We can talk about what we might want to do."

"That's a good idea."

They went back out to the wagons. "You find out anything?" Amos asked.

"Been here and gone," James said.

"Sorry to hear that."

James looked puzzled. "It just occurred to me: Don't you always have to sort of ease into towns before you let folks see you? You rode in here like you were in a military parade."

"I haven't been here before. You have no idea how relaxing it is to enter a town and not be looking over your shoulder."

"I'll bet."

A distinguished-looking Spanish man came up to James and said, "Well, my goodness. It's you, isn't it?"

"Do I know you?" James asked.

"No, but I know you." He removed his flat-brimmed hat with the gold braid around the rim as he extended his hand. "I am Don Carlos Rafael Montoya. I run the bank of the Ranchos de Taos." The man wore an elegant Spanish-cut suit with a waist-length jacket and black braiding down the trouser seam.

James took the hand. "That's quite a mouthful."

"It is indeed. My friends call me Rafael—you may do the same." He made a dismissive gesture with his free hand.

"How is it that you know me, Mr. Montoya?"

"Your brother said you would look just like him, only be dressed as a farmer. His words, not mine. I had no idea the resemblance would be so strong."

"We do look a lot like each other, all right."

"I thought it might be about time for you to arrive, so I have been carrying this in my pocket." He pulled an official-looking paper with a blue backing sheet from an inside pocket of his jacket.

Montoya unfolded the document. "Your brother transacted a land deal with me on your behalf and instructed me to give you the papers when you showed up. He said I would know you by your resemblance to him, and by the fact that you would be traveling in the company of two lovely ladies."

He tipped his hat to the women. "I'm sorry to

have conducted business before I introduced myself. I fear the startling resemblance between Mr. Campbell and his brother rather unsettled me." He introduced himself to the ladies, bowing deeply, then to Amos and Joseph. Such courtly manners were a new and exciting experience for Ma and Mary Jane.

James paid no attention and began looking at the document. "These papers have *my* name on them."

The banker turned back to him, replacing his hat at a jaunty angle. "They do indeed. I gathered from your brother that he intended for you two to go into partnership, but as he had to move on, he apparently meant for you to take possession of the land. He wanted it to be in your name in case anything happened to him."

James looked puzzled. "I don't mean to look no gift horse in the mouth, but how do I know these titles are any good? From what we've been hearing, there are all sorts of land disputes around here."

"A very astute observation, but the office of the surveyor general is working to clear up those disputes, and the title on this property has already been affirmed. No matter how the litigation in question may be resolved, this title is secure."

James looked dazed. "This is pretty hard to wrap my mind around."

"What is it, James?" Ma asked.

"Ross has gone and bought eighty acres with a house on it."

Ma's mouth fell open. "*Eighty acres?* That's a lot

bigger than our place back in Tennessee."

"Yes'm." James looked at the banker. "We used to farm a little hardscrabble patch on the sides of the Cumberland Mountains."

The banker nodded to show his understanding. "A hard life. I think this will be an improvement."

Ma was starting to come to grips with it. "That's a lot of land to work with two mules."

"Yes'm, it is," James said. "But we ought to be able to make do. I wonder what come over Ross?"

Ma had never given up on the fact that there was good in both of her sons, and that belief had never wavered, no matter what Ross had done. "He promised to help out. I expect it just took him a while to be able to do it."

"I wonder where he got the money?" Suspicion was growing in James's mind that it might be ill-gotten wealth. If it was, he didn't want any part of it.

"He paid in gold dust," Montoya said. "I expect he had some success up in the gold fields."

That surprised James. "You don't say?" The idea of Ross doing any kind of physical labor didn't sound right. Still, there was a difference in digging with a plow and digging for riches. "I guess it's all right then. How do we find this place?"

Montoya took a step back and made a sweeping gesture with his hand. "I have a two-seat surrey over here. I would be honored to take you out and show it to you."

James turned, "You be okay in an open surrey, Ma?"

She knew what he meant. "I'll be fine. I haven't had a problem since we got back inside all of these wonderful trees."

"Y'all go on," Amos said. "We'll take your wagon over to the wagon yard. We're going to go ahead and set up camp."

Thirty-four

*L*arge cottonwood trees stood all over the valley, testimony to the abundant rainfall and the plentiful water. The mountains stood on three sides, with the north open as far as the eye could see. The mountains were covered thickly with tall evergreens.

The property in question was southeast of the village. The land had a gentle slope to it, leading up to another of the pink adobe buildings seen all over the community. This one backed up to the edge of the mountain.

As it came into view, Ma said, "Are you telling me that's it?"

The banker smiled. "Yes, ma'am, it is."

"It's so big."

"It's not as big as it looks. It is actually four rooms built around a little courtyard. Our people are quite fond of courtyards, you see."

"A courtyard?" Ma was having trouble picturing it. "In the middle of the house? Don't that beat all?"

The surrey pulled up in front of the house. The way the big cottonwoods grew around it, the house was nicely shaded during most of the day. There was a large double front door made of heavy, carved wood. The banker led the group inside. "It was owned by an old couple who died intestate."

"What does that mean?" James asked.

The banker was patient, now that he understood the people with whom he was dealing. He was drawn to the gentle family, with their charming naïveté. "It means they died with no will and no family to leave it to. The title, which as I said earlier is clear, reverted to the bank. You don't have to keep the furnishings, of course."

Mary Jane's eyes were as large as saucers. "I never saw anything so grand."

Montoya knew that would be the response. These were the kind of people he wanted to see settle in the area. Honest and hardworking, these folks would become deeply rooted in the community.

He walked to the center of the room. They followed as if they were touring a museum. "This home was built in the style of the area. This is the great room. Food is prepared at this end," he said, pointing to his right. "They used to cook in that fireplace before they got the wood stove. Had it shipped in, the latest thing."

Ma had stepped to the stove, and she now ran her hand over it lovingly. Montoya continued: "They did no entertaining, so there is no formal dining room. They ate in the kitchen, and the room is open to this seating area on the other end."

They walked to the other end of the room. It was furnished with two couches of bright fabric. The arms, legs, and exposed wood were square and ornately carved in the same pattern as the doors of the entryway; the pattern was repeated on a large cabinet. Montoya pointed to a door. "The remainder of the house is divided so that each of the sides is a separate bedroom; more than that, each is like a small home unto itself. I assume your brother was interested in that feature so that you and your wife had one, there was another one for your mother, and I'm sure he intended the other for him when he joined you."

Before James could correct him on the wife part of his comments, the banker turned to throw open one of the French doors that lined the room. It opened onto a beautiful little courtyard, which was paved with flagstone rocks. It had a well in the center and was shaded by a couple of cottonwood trees. "Each of the rooms opens onto the courtyard in this manner. It's quite a pretty little house."

"Little house," Ma said quietly. "Every room is bigger than our entire house back in the hills."

"Can you imagine having a whole room to sleep in by yourself?" James said.

Montoya went on with the tour, enjoying their response. "Each room has a separate fireplace, of course." He stopped to give them his most gracious Latin smile. "If you are not familiar with them, these adobe houses retain heat quite well, yet stay comfortably cool in the summer."

"This is a wonderment," James said. "I can't believe it."

"In my opinion, your brother made quite a nice choice," said Montoya. "You may move in any time you wish; it is yours. I will take you back for your wagon and see that you have an account set up at the store so that you obtain the provisions you need."

"It don't seem real," Ma said. "I surely have to be dreaming."

"So much for us having to talk about the future," James said.

Santa Fe was the big sister of Taos. Square adobe buildings surrounded a lush green plaza shaded by mature trees. In the center stood a large gazebo where a number of social functions were staged. There was a peaceful feel to it as Ross walked his horse past the Church of Our Lady of Guadalupe and into the plaza area. "I could get used to this," Ross said to no one in particular.

As usual, he tied up his horse and went into the saloon to get the lay of the land. This one had a south-of-the-border feel with bright serapes and ornate sombreros decorating the walls.

Ross took a table and ordered a drink, then a steak. He settled in to do some serious eating.

A thunder arose in the street. The unique mix of creaking leather, rumbling axles, stamping horses' hooves, and the squeal of the wooden brake being applied to the steel rim of the wheels indicated that the stagecoach had pulled into town. A faint cloud of dust wafted into the room.

A couple of passengers ventured in, and a short time later the dust-covered driver and guard followed them. No sooner were they in the door than Ross called them over and ordered them a drink and a meal. In a country starved for information, those who handled these rigs had more of that particular commodity than anyone, and as a result they seldom had to buy a drink or a meal.

"Rough trip?" Ross asked, as they used their hats to brush the dust from their clothes before they took their seats. Ross was glad he had finished his steak as he watched the dust settle over everything.

"No harder'n usual," the driver said, extending his hand. "My name's Les, short for Lester." He grinned. "This here's Roger."

"Good to meet you boys." The barkeep arrived with two mugs and a couple of steaks that overflowed the plates on every side. The stagecoach hands knew what the meal was buying and were glad to oblige. They spoke around huge bites of food, making the words hard to distinguish.

They passed on the usual gossip, Ross asking questions until he could work the conversation around to the topics he was really interested in exploring. Finally he asked, "Say, you boys run into a feller named Slocum on this trip?"

"Bulldog?" Les nodded. "Sure, seen him on the trail a ways back. We was carrying a note for him, but he'd already seen it. Stopped and jawed with him a couple of minutes anyway 'fore the passengers got to fussing about it. People are just in too big a hurry." Using his steak knife, he pointed toward the people seated across the room. They were not disguising their eagerness to board the coach and get under way.

"I was hoping to catch up to him," Ross lied. "He's an old friend."

Les sawed at the meat like he was cutting a fence post, shaving off a chunk that might have served as one. Before he stuffed it into his mouth, he said, "You're gonna have to wait until he gets back from that border war. All them ranger fellers got called up."

That news set well with Ross. *So I don't have to be in a big hurry.* That was a relief. Maybe he would just stay around here for a while.

Another guy at the bar called over to them, "Les, didn't I hear tell there was some trouble over to Elizabethtown?"

Les gave a prodigious swallow before he answered. "They had another robbery."

"They catch the one that done it?"

"No, but when we come through Taos, there was a couple of guys right stirred up. Seems they'd seen the varmint that took their gold and was headed back to Elizabethtown to get help to go string him up."

The man looked interested. "You don't say."

"Seems this jasper ain't too smart. Used the

money to buy himself a place out of town and settle down."

"Right in the shadow of the place where he stole the money? That don't seem right. They sure it was him?"

"Saw him clear as day. He walked right by them and acted like he'd never seen them before in his life."

"Why didn't they just brace him then?"

"They say this galoot is a hand with a gun, and them old fools couldn't hit the broad side of a barn with a twelve-gauge if they was on the inside. They did the sensible thing and went for help." He turned back to his host. "Did you hear about that, stranger? Stranger?"

The chair where he had been sitting was empty. Ross was already spurring his horse across the plaza on his way out of town.

Thirty-five

Slocum sat in the white army tent. He struggled to write a letter, the first he had ever composed other than some cryptic reports posted back to headquarters.

"I take pen in hand," he wrote. *That's silly*, he thought. *Of course I have my pen in my hand; how else would I be writing this?*

He went through draft after draft, the pile of wadded paper stacking up at his feet. He finally ended up with a letter that he signed with a flourish and sealed to send.

Dear Miss McMinn,

I hope this letter finds you in good health. You have been on my mind constantly as we have been sitting around camp, training recruits for the upcoming campaign. After much thought, my mind is finally clear concerning my feelings for you.

I care for you a great deal, but I have a jealous mistress, and her name is Texas. I thought to walk away and put her behind me, but she called, and I answered. I understand now that I will always answer her call, but I am sure you know that already. I saw it in your eyes when we last parted. What I might want to do and what I must do are not the same thing.

I know you care for me too. I don't know if you love me, or if I love you, as we have not progressed to the stage to find out. It is clear we will never know, but it is my sincere hope that we will always remain friends.

Your obedient servant,
Sgt. John David Slocum

"Sergeant John David Slocum!" Mary Jane was furious as she read the letter. "He not only signed his complete name, but his rank? I cannot believe it." The two were sitting in the living area of their new house.

Ma smiled. "But isn't he only saying what you had already decided?"

"Yes, but it's just so ... so ... cold."

"Is that it, or did you simply want to be the one who broke it off?"

"Oh, maybe." She wadded up the letter and drew back to throw it into the small morning fire. Her hand froze in that position, she reconsidered, and then she smoothed out the paper to put it away.

Ma watched her. "So where does this leave things? Have you given up on chasing Ross?"

"It's pointless. Without James to lead the way, I would have no idea where to look. Besides, I've been near him a couple of times now, and he has shown no interest whatsoever. I think I just had a girlish crush, and he never returned it, not at all."

Ma leaned over to give her a pat on the forearm. "I've thought that for some time, but you didn't want to hear it. I'm pleased you're realizing it."

"No more than I wanted to admit the truth about John David. I thought I had three men to choose from, but I don't think I ever did."

"You still have James."

"Do I? Do I love James, or would I just be settling?" The question mark she added with her eyes was clear, compelling. "I don't want him if that's all he is to me, just second choice."

Ma put her mending aside. This was getting serious. "We talked about what love really is." Mary Jane's emotions seemed to be on the edge, as if about to boil over into tears or anger; Ma couldn't decide which.

"Yes, we did, and you are right. I just have to figure out if what I feel for James is really love. I wish he'd court me or chase after me. I don't want us to just drift together as a matter of convenience. Maybe I should move into town and get a job. Make him pursue me if he wants me."

"I don't think that's necessary."

"Really? What right do I have to be here? It was

different when we were traveling together, but the traveling has ended. You are making a home here, a home I have no right to be in."

The direction Mary Jane's thoughts were going began to trouble Ma more and more. "You're as much a daughter to me as if you had been born to me."

"I feel the same, Ma, but you know what I mean. I need to work it out with James. We need to get serious if we're courting or really decide we are going to be brother and sister if we aren't. I could live here as a member of the family, but I can't stay as things are now."

"I understand that. You two need to share some plain talk. You need to put it all out on the table."

"I don't want to talk. I'm tired of doing all the work. If he wants me, he has to take the initiative. Then we can decide whether there's anything between us or not. If he doesn't take the initiative, I'm going to find somebody who will."

Zeke and Rufus came rushing into the saloon back at Elizabethtown. "We seen him! We seen him!"

Slade moved over and poured them a drink. "Who have you seen? What are you boys talking about?"

Men crowded around as Zeke drained his glass and pushed it back toward Slade for more. "That varmint that lifted our dust, that's who. He passed us on the sidewalk in Taos, cool as a snowdrift. He even had the gall to speak to us as if he'd never seen us before in his life. I was so mad I coulda chewed horseshoe nails."

Slade said, "Why didn't you gun him down?"

Zeke got wide eyed. "Are you kidding me? You think he wears them two pistols just for show? I ain't no gunslinger."

"You know, Zeke," Rufus said, "I don't recall him having them pistols on when we brushed by him."

"Don't be stirring mud into the water. He prob'bly had one tucked into his belt or somethin'. He wouldn't be out without 'em."

Rufus nodded. "You're prob'bly right, but I'll tell you one thing, boys—we don't intend to let him get away with it. We come to get that posse back together. We want to do this legal like."

Zeke agreed. "Yeah, and we want to do it with a dozen guns, not just a couple of old coots with rifles."

The idea that the man who had robbed their friends hadn't even bothered to leave the area infuriated the rest of the miners as much as it had Zeke and Rufus. It took no time to raise a posse and get them saddled up to head for Taos, determined to set things right.

Ross made the best time he could without killing his horse, but even at the reduced pace the animal was starting to lather and breathe heavily. He stopped, used some handfuls of grass to rub the laboring horse, and walked it a bit to cool it down. He had been talking to himself ever since he left Santa Fe.

"I've got to be going nuts. I'm about to kill a good horse trying to get someplace I don't even want to be. This is the break I've been looking for. Those miners are going to go over there and find James, probably toss him in the calaboose for a while, and as far as the law is concerned, I'll cease to exist." His free hand made extravagant gestures, fluttering like a bird. "I'll be free and clear as long as I keep my head down. It's the chance of a lifetime."

It wasn't his nature to care about other people. He had lived his entire life looking out for number one. He was naturally good natured and gregarious, as long as it didn't go against his own best interest. When it did, he could be counted upon to always do what appeared to be best for him.

He swung back into the saddle and jerked his heels. "So why am I jumping back on this horse? It don't make no sense. Ain't like I care whether they get that knothead brother of mine or not. I got it all figured out; I know what I want to do. So why am I riding?"

Thirty-six

*J*ames was breaking in a new plow and breaking ground in a new field at the same time. It was too early to plant; of course, he just needed to do it, to take possession of the land by working it. He was plowing up roots and rocks, clearing the land for when it would come time for him to plant. For years he had done it woodenly, automatically, just going through the motions, doing what he had to do. Those days were gone. Now working the land felt good; the smell of the fresh earth filled his nose and pleased him, as he had never thought it would. This was *his* land.

When the time came to do so, James had already decided he would plant corn and other vegetables for their own use and to sell in town. He calculated that the rainfall would sustain such a crop, and if not, he had already figured out how to tap into the nearby mountain stream to divert irrigation water to the crop.

He wrestled the plow, reins looped over his neck and under one shoulder. His old mule, Henry, knew the drill. He would have to start breaking Zachariah to the plow, but he wasn't in a mood to do that yet. It was a totally different skill to pull a plow as opposed to pulling a wagon. Not hard, just different.

Somehow the act of tilling the land finally began to make it feel like home. So far it had felt as if he were staying in someone else's house. Another reason he wanted to do a little plowing was to allow him to get away from the house and have time to think, about Mary Jane. His competition for her attention had disappeared, yet nothing had changed. They were more like brother and sister, even more so now that she had a room of her own to which she could escape.

Ma had alerted him before he left the barn. Mary Jane wanted to be courted. He had to take things in hand, or he would lose her. He had never gone court-ing before and was unsure how to proceed. He decided he would get cleaned up, get a big handful of wildflowers from the upper meadow, and—

A voice startled him. "Did you think you could hide here right under our noses?"

James had been so deep in thought that he hadn't even noticed the group of riders quietly moving up to the fence. The man speaking was old, with the look of a miner.

"I beg your pardon, but I don't think plowing my own field qualifies as hiding. Besides that, why would I want to hide?"

"If'n you was a real farmer you wouldn't be turning over a field this time of year. Did you think this was far enough away from the gold fields that you'd be safe?" the old man asked. Several of the men dismounted, jumped the fence, and grabbed James roughly.

James tried to shake off the rough hands. "Let go of me! Safe from what? I have no idea what you're talking about."

The old man didn't jump the fence but stepped through the rails. Another old man followed him. "How stupid do you think we are?" the first one continued. "You think we don't know where you got the money to buy this place? Me'n Rufus here done found out in town you paid for it with gold dust. *Our gold dust.*"

James looked pained. *So that's it. I should have known Ross wouldn't have come by the money honestly. I got stars in my eyes, and I should have known better.* "I think I'm beginning to understand. Somebody robbed you?"

"How far you gonna try to play this hand?" Rufus asked. "It wasn't somebody—it was you."

"No, it wasn't, but I think I know who it was. I have a twin brother. He bought this land and put the title in my name. I should have known better than to accept it."

The first old man showed a toothless smile with no humor in it. "That's all right 'cause it ain't me,

Zeke, that's gonna hang you; it'll be my evil twin hanging yore evil twin."

"No, really, I know it's hard to believe, but—"

The men started dragging him toward the cottonwood trees at the edge of the field. "Wait, wait! Listen to me!" He fought to escape them, but to no avail.

The commotion brought Ma and Mary Jane running from the house. "Stop that," Ma yelled. "What do you think you're doing?" Two men headed the women off and restrained them.

"Ma'am, this ain't something you want to see," said Zeke. Then he turned to two men and said, "You boys take them back to the house."

They started dragging them back toward the house. A man threw a rope with a noose in it over a tree limb. Ma caught sight of it and screamed. She tore loose from the arms restraining her and rushed the group. When they grabbed her again, she began to scratch and claw.

"Can't you boys handle an old ninety-pound woman?" Rufus shouted.

The men again started back toward the house with them. Rough hands tied James's hands behind his back and jerked the noose tight on his neck. "You want to make peace with your Maker?" Zeke asked.

"I tell you, you have the wrong man."

"You gonna play that twin thing out to the end?"

"He's telling you the truth," Ma screamed, getting farther away. "I had twin sons. Whatever you think he did, it had to have been his brother, Ross. We haven't been away from James for any time at all since we left Tennessee."

Zeke removed his hat and held it against his chest. "Ma'am, that's right admirable, backing yore boy's story thataway, but you shoulda settled on something a mite more believable. I'm sorry for your sake, but he's earned this right enough. Are you boys gonna be able to get them back in that house or what?"

The men began to muscle them back toward the house again. Mary Jane looked over and said, "Ma, what happens if an airtight crock of peaches gets too hot?"

"Lands, child, it can explode like a bomb. Why?"

"Because it just occurred to me where I set the one I had in my hands when we ran out of the house—on the edge of the stove. I think we're about to have a diversion."

One of the men said, "A diversion ain't gonna do you no good; we ain't letting loose of you. May spook them boys into action back there though."

"Oh no," Mary Jane said. *Is it possible I really* am *a jinx? All of these things that keep happening ...*

Behind them Zeke turned back to James. "I asked you if you wanted to make yore peace or not."

James lifted his chin. "I try to stay in good stead with the Lord. I don't need any last-minute effort."

Zeke replaced the old misshapen hat on his balding head. "You call lifting my gold pokes staying in good stead with Him? You got a mighty liberal religion, friend."

"He didn't lift your poke. I did." The men spun around to see a man who looked like James holding a gun on them. They looked at him, turned to look at

James, then repeated the double take, back and forth.

"Well, I'll be hornswoggled," Zeke said.

"This is my twin brother, Ross, like Ma told you," said James. "Don't you feel almighty silly?"

Zeke looked at the guns, the clothing. "I do fer a fact, but if'n you two are twins, that means that rope will fit his neck as good as yore's."

Ross pointed his pistol menacingly at the men holding James. "Nobody is putting a noose around my neck, but you are going to take it off his and untie his hands right now. Turn him around where you don't have to go behind him to do it."

One man lifted the noose up over James's head. As the rope came loose, the jar of peaches exploded exactly as Ma had predicted with a sound like a rifle shot. The man holding James spun him around and, using him for a shield, drew his pistol.

James realized what was happening and elbowed him in the nose. The gun went off, hitting Zeke in the back. The old man fell to his knees but managed to draw his own gun to fire into Ross before he toppled over on his face.

Everyone grabbed at their weapons, and Ross, ignoring his wound, began firing with both hands, backing away. These were miners, not gunfighters, and several men went down. Ross was hit again but dropped to his knees, still firing.

"Stop! Everyone stop!" James screamed, rushing the men. Ma and Mary Jane broke loose and began to run toward Ross as he slumped to the ground. The firing stopped. No one seemed to know what had happened or what to do next.

James reached Ross before the ladies got there and rolled his brother over, his head resting in his lap. He looked down at him with tears in his eyes. "This ain't like you, Ross, putting yourself on the line for somebody else."

Ross smiled weakly. "It appears I wasn't very good at it anyway, was I?"

"You saved my bacon. They had me measured for a long drop on a short rope."

Ross looked puzzled. "Who started the shooting?"

Mary Jane looked down at him. "It wasn't a who, it was a what."

"Huh?"

"A crock of peaches got too hot and exploded. Actually it was because—"

Ross held up a hand to silence her. "I know, I know, and you were nowhere near any of it." He looked up at his brother. "Now do you believe me that she's a jinx?" Ross started to laugh, then grasped his chest in pain. "No matter, that little sideshow kept you out of it, even if it done me in. I never done a lick of good in my whole life, but I couldn't let them string you up for something I done. I'm glad it turned them away from you."

Ma said, "Is he ...?"

James nodded, but Ross answered, "Ma, they've killed me. I'm sorry I've been such a disappointment to you."

She sat down beside him. "You weren't a disappointment. I just wish things had gone better for you."

"Ross, you're right," James said. "You're hit bad.

You'd best spend your time getting right with the Lord."

Ross shook his head and went into a coughing spasm that brought intense pain from his wounds. It took him a moment to collect himself. "It's too late. All these years I've made fun of your religion, but really I envied you for it. It always made you strong, stronger than I was. I could always lick you in a fight, but your strength was inside, where it counted."

"It's never too late, Ross. Jesus saved a thief on the cross, seconds before he died. If he could receive salvation, you can too."

"I've done too much to be forgiven."

"That's just it, Ross. We can't earn our way to heaven. It's a gift. Jesus died to cover our sins. Whether we've led a pretty good life or a really bad one, we're all sinners. None of us deserves what He offers us: forgiveness and salvation."

"You really believe that?"

"With all my heart."

"Listen to him, Ross," Ma said. "He's giving it to you straight. It's never too late."

He searched her face. If there was anyone in the world he trusted without question, it was Ma. "What do I do?"

"You believe you're a sinner?" James asked.

He looked back at his brother. "As bad as they come."

"You believe Jesus died for your sins and rose again the third day?"

Ross was getting weaker, and his voice was

getting so low that James had to get close to hear. There wasn't much time. "I've heard you and Ma talk about it, and I don't understand it, but I believe it. I don't know why He would though."

"You just have to believe and ask Him to come into your heart and save you." James led Ross in a prayer; then he said, "You really believe what you just said?"

"Yes, but I can't believe that's all there is to it."

"That's it, though I'm afraid you're going to have a lot to answer for when you stand in front of the judgment seat."

"I'm not looking forward to that."

"Don't worry. Jesus is going to be standing there speaking on your behalf, saying He paid for your sins. You believe that, don't you, Ross? Ross?"

He was gone.

Thirty-seven

The men had paid no attention to what was going on with James and Ross. They were busy tending to their own wounded. Most wounds were slight, but Zeke was hurt bad. He was also running out of time. Leaving the ladies to mourn for Ross, James went to him to see if there was anything he could do.

"I tried to hang you, and here you are trying to help me?" Zeke rasped.

"It doesn't look like there's anything I can do."

"No, I'm a goner, and that's a fact. Can you raise me up a bit? I want to say something to your mother."

Zeke grimaced at the pain as they helped him raise up a bit. "Ma'am," he croaked. "I done killed one of your boys and nearly killed the other one. There ain't nothing I can do to make up for that, but I want all these boys to bear witness for me. This here place was bought with my money, but here in a few minutes, I ain't gonna have no use for land or money anymore. I release any claim I might have on this place and the gold that bought it; and not only that, what dust and belongings I've got back at the camp, I want delivered to this lady. I know it won't balance up the debt, but I want to go out with a clear conscience."

"I'll see to it, Zeke," Rufus said, "and that goes for any part I might have in this too."

Tears came into Ma's eyes, but she couldn't find any words.

James looked down at Zeke. "Are you a Christian?"

Zeke smiled. "Got my name in the Lamb's Book a long time ago, son, though I ain't lived like I should. Reckon I'll have some explaining to do, but the Lord won't turn His back on me."

James wiped the sweat from the old man's face with his bandanna. "Do you mind if I say a prayer for you?"

"Son, I'd take that mighty kindly."

James kneeled and began to pray. Somewhere in the middle of his prayer, Zeke made the trip home.

They buried Ross and Zeke together in a clearing just up the mountain, overlooking the valley. Mary Jane said, "They killed each other—do you think this is right?"

James smiled and said in a gentle voice, "I 'spect they've made their peace by now."

They stood there for some time, not speaking, gazing at the two mounds of dirt. Finally Mary Jane said, "I'm going to have to leave."

James spun around to face her. "What?"

"Ross said it plain. He was right all along; I just wasn't willing to admit it. I'm a jinx. Just thinking about it kept me awake all last night. I know my carelessness was what touched off that terrible fight in the field. No doubt about it. Then I remembered other things: the restaurant, the store, things that always happen around me. I've always thought people were just careless. Last night I finally understood; they aren't careless when I'm not around. It's me. I've been causing it all."

She buried her face in her hands and began to sob. "I can't saddle you and Ma with that kind of misfortune. I have to leave."

James took her in his arms. "Don't be silly. Ma and I figured out some time ago that not all the helpful things you do work out the way you have in mind. Haven't you noticed we haven't had any misfortunes since we've been here at this place, not counting the peaches, of course. Ma and I just kinda watch out behind you to see if there are any loose ends. Ma woulda caught the thing about the peaches if she hadn't been so upset. It's just a little game to add spice to our lives. You're making way too big a thing out of it."

She looked up at him with her big brown eyes moist and warm. "You've known all along?"

He laughed. "I wouldn't say all along, but for a spell now."

"Why didn't you say anything?"

"You weren't ready to hear it."

"I don't know why you were willing to go to so much trouble for me."

"I ain't never had no choice, the way I feel about you."

What was he trying to say? Why couldn't he ever come right out with things? "What do you mean, James? You've got to speak it plain."

"I'm willing. It ain't that I mind telling you what's in my heart; I'm just almighty bad at it."

"Let me ask you flat out. James Campbell, do you love me?"

"The easiest thing to do would be to just say yes, but I reckon I don't know. I ain't never been in love before. I know I go to bed thinking of you at night and wake up with you on my mind in the morning. I think of you as I work, and every time I see something, my first thought is wanting to share it with you. I look at you, and I get this knot in my stomach. I don't know whether it's love or not, but I can't imagine what my life would be like without you in it."

"I don't know whether that's love or not either, James, but I'd sure settle for it."

"How about if I go get me a handful of flowers and come calling at your door? Ma said you'd like that. We can go on courting as long as you like."

"That sounds nice," Mary Jane said with a twinkle in her eye. "But how about if we just find Ma and go get ourselves hitched instead?"

James threw his head back and laughed. "That suits me plumb down to the ground, and I know just where to find me a preacher. Reckon this is why Amos said he needed to come this way with us?"

READERS' GUIDE

For Personal Reflection
or Group Discussion

Readers' Guide

*I*n *Brother's Keeper*, the main characters are twin brothers whose natures couldn't be more different. The boys were raised in the same home environment yet choose vastly different paths for their lives. Conflict revolves around their interaction with Mary Jane, a guileless and strangely accident-prone young woman, and one another. These questions will help you discover the life lessons that are hidden in this little tale, prompting you to think about yourself and those you love.

1. The title *Brother's Keeper* suggests that one brother is going to be looking out for the other. At what point in the story did you discover that? What was your reaction when you discovered which brother would do the keeping? How much of an obligation do you feel you have to be your brother's keeper?

2. How did you feel about James taking his mother and striking out in search of his twin brother? Did it strike you as a fool's errand, or as an appropriate reaction to the circumstances? When Mary Jane invited herself along, what was your reaction?

3. How does stress affect your ability to make solid life decisions? Which characters in this novel try to make decisions while under stress?

4. Mary Jane is oblivious to the disaster she leaves behind in her wake. Do you believe there is really such a thing as a jinx or jonah? How would you treat someone who exhibited those characteristics?

5. Losing loved ones can be one of the biggest trials of our faith. Mary Jane feels that she has lost her faith as a result of such a loss. Think of some times in your own life when you experienced similar feelings. How did you deal with it? How did you feel about Mary Jane's journey to reclaim her faith?

6. Ross was raised by a Christian mother, but turned from that heritage to living outside the law. What do you think caused him to choose that life? How did the faith of his mother and brother affect him? How did you feel about his status at the end of the novel? What application can you draw from that?

7. Ross was a rascal, no doubt about it. Does he have any redeeming qualities that drew you to him? If so, what are they?

8. In this novel, Ma is plagued with agoraphobia, though they didn't have a name for it then. She was unaware of it until she left the close confines of the mountain forestland. How must it feel to have a fear of open spaces and suddenly find yourself in a wagon traveling through rough and wild territory?

9. The racial riot in Memphis is a documented historical event. How did James's background as a mountain boy who had never been exposed to racism or the issues of racial equality affect his attitude? How did you feel about his reaction to the events in Memphis?

10. How did you feel about the author's use of shifting scenes and characters to keep you abreast of the actions of all the characters? What was your reaction when the various storylines converged toward the end of the novel? Were you presented with a few surprises?

11. How did you feel about Mary Jane's choice of the man she loved? Did she choose as you thought she would? Why or why not?

12. What does the relationship between Mary Jane and the two brothers tell us about relationships in our own lives?

13. How did you feel about the larger-than-life Ranger? What role does he play in this novel? Were you impressed by his dogged determination and devotion to duty or did you find him inflexible and unwilling to change?

14. Did you feel it was out of character for Ross to ride back when he knew what his brother faced? Or was that his character all along?

15. In the light of the questions posed, what aspects of this story caused you to reflect on your own life and the decisions you have made?

About the Author

Terry Burns is a fifth-generation Irish storyteller who is also a fourth-generation Texas teller of tall tales. He says telling stories "comes as natural as breathing." He also says he is honoring a commitment to try to provide some good Christian entertainment and, at the same time, in his small way, to make his words count for the Lord.

He has a new line of inspirational fiction set in the old west from RiverOak Books, and the lead book, *Mysterious Ways,* was nominated for American Christian Fiction Writers Book of the Year. *Trails of the Dime Novel* is out from Echelon Press and in audio from JBS Publications. *To Keep a Promise,* a trade paperback from the Fiction Works, was a finalist for the Eppie award and nominated for the Willa award. A second title, *Don't I Know You?* is from the same publisher.

He has published short stories in the following collections: Coastal Villages Press's *"From the Heart: Stories of Love and Friendship,"* a second volume titled *More Stories of Love and Friendship* from the same publisher, and one titled *Living by Faith* from Obadiah Press. Terry has a small book of cowboy poetry titled *Cowboys Don't Read Poetry.* More on the author and his available works can be found at the author's Web site at www.terryburns.net.

Additional copies of *BROTHER'S KEEPER* are available
wherever good books are sold.

If you have enjoyed this book,
or if it has had an impact on your life,
we would like to hear from you.

Please contact us at:

RIVEROAK BOOKS
Cook Communications Ministries, Dept. 201
4050 Lee Vance View
Colorado Springs, CO 80918
Or
visit our Web site: www.cookministries.com

RIVEROAK®
Good News in Fiction